LEARNIN

The door of the cottage was ajar so the Earl opened it and looked inside.

There was no one in the kitchen, but there was however the sound of voices on the other side of the passage where he thought Kristina must be.

He was just about to knock on the door when a woman saw him and withdrew. He heard her say,

"His Lordship is here, my Lady."

The Earl waited.

A few minutes later, Kristina entered the room carrying a baby in her arms wrapped in a white shawl and she walked towards the Earl holding the infant very carefully.

"Here is a new member of your flock," she smiled. "You must admit he is a very good-looking baby."

As the child had only just been born, the Earl found it difficult to decide what his looks would be like in later life.

At the same time he was sure he had never seen anything quite so delightful as Kristina with a child in her arms. The scene made him think of the picture books of the Madonna which his mother had read to him when he was a little boy.

THE BARBARA CARTLAND PINK COLLECTION

Titles in this series

LEARNING TO LOVE

BARBARA CARTLAND

Barbaracartland.com Ltd

Printed and bound in Great Britain by CLE Print Ltd,
St Ives, Cambridgeshire

THE BARBARA CARTLAND PINK COLLECTION

Barbara Cartland was the most prolific bestselling author in the history of the world. She was frequently in the Guinness Book of Records for writing more books in a year than any other living author. In fact her most amazing literary feat was when her publishers asked for more Barbara Cartland romances, she doubled her output from 10 books a year to over 20 books a year, when she was 77.

She went on writing continuously at this rate for 20 years and wrote her last book at the age of 97, thus completing 400 books between the ages of 77 and 97.

Her publishers finally could not keep up with this phenomenal output, so at her death she left 160 unpublished manuscripts, something again that no other author has ever achieved.

Now the exciting news is that these 160 original unpublished Barbara Cartland books are ready for publication and they will be published by Barbaracartland.com exclusively on the internet, as the web is the best possible way to reach so many Barbara Cartland readers around the world.

The 160 books will be published monthly and will be numbered in sequence.

The series is called the Pink Collection as a tribute to Barbara Cartland whose favourite colour was pink and it became very much her trademark over the years.

The Barbara Cartland Pink Collection is published only on the internet. Log on to www.barbaracartland.com to find out how you can purchase the books monthly as they are published, and take out a subscription that will ensure that all subsequent editions are delivered to you by mail order to your home.

If you do not have access to a computer you can write for information about the Pink Collection to the following address :

Barbara Cartland.com Ltd.
Camfield Place,
Hatfield,
Hertfordshire AL9 6JE
United Kingdom.

Telephone : +44 (0)1707 642629
Fax :   +44 (0)1707 663041

THE LATE DAME BARBARA CARTLAND

Barbara Cartland who sadly died in May 2000 at the age of nearly 99 was the world's most famous romantic novelist who wrote 723 books in her lifetime with worldwide sales of over 1 billion copies and her books were translated into 36 different languages.

As well as romantic novels, she wrote historical biographies, 6 autobiographies, theatrical plays, books of advice on life, love, vitamins and cookery. She also found time to be a political speaker and television and radio personality.

She wrote her first book at the age of 21 and this was called Jigsaw. It became an immediate bestseller and sold 100,000 copies in hardback and was translated into 6 different languages. She wrote continuously throughout her life, writing bestsellers for an astonishing 76 years. Her books have always been immensely popular in the United States, where in 1976 her current books were at numbers 1 & 2 in the B. Dalton bestsellers list, a feat never achieved before or since by any author.

Barbara Cartland became a legend in her own lifetime and will be best remembered for her wonderful romantic novels, so loved by her millions of readers throughout the world.

Her books will always be treasured for their moral message, her pure and innocent heroines, her good looking and dashing heroes and above all her belief that the power of love is more important than anything else in everyone's life.

"We must always believe that love can conquer all."
Barbara Cartland

CHAPTER ONE
1880

The Earl of Cariston walked into White's Club in St. James's Street. The Club's porter having welcomed him politely informed him,

"The Club Secretary, my Lord, would like to have a word with you when you have time."

The Earl did not reply because he knew exactly what the Secretary wanted to have a word with him about. He had not paid his subscription for the simple reason that he had not enough money to make the payment.

He walked into the morning room and seeing a friend of his at the far end, he walked across to join him.

Lord Shield looked up in surprise.

"Hallo, Michael," he exclaimed. "I thought you were in the country."

The Earl sat down rather heavily in the chair next to his.

"I came up to London," he told him, "to see my Solicitor."

"Trouble?" Lord Shield enquired.

"Very bad trouble," the Earl replied, "and I would be grateful if you would stand me a drink because I literally cannot afford one."

His friend did not argue. He merely signalled to a Steward and ordered a bottle of champagne.

"I am very sorry for you, Michael," he said when they were alone. "Are things worse than they have ever been?"

"Far, far worse!"

He spoke with a note of despair in his voice which his companion could not fail to miss.

The two young men had been at Oxford together and had then joined the same Regiment. They had fought in the Sudan and spent some very uncomfortable months during the troubles in Abyssinia.

When the Earl had inherited his title he had resigned his commission in the Army and returned home. Lord Shield had done the same six months later.

Whenever they had the chance they met, as both of them owned large estates in the country.

Now as they waited for the champagne to arrive, Lord Shield was recalling that last year had been a particularly bad harvest and every landowner had been affected.

He had heard the story that the Earl was having a particularly difficult time on his estate.

There was silence for a little while and then Lord Shield said,

"Tell me the worst. You know, Michael, that I will help you if I possibly can."

"Nobody can help me!" the Earl responded gloomily. "I am completely finished. The best thing I could do would be to put a bullet through my head!"

"Don't be so ridiculous! It cannot be as bad as that!"

"It is worse!"

"Tell me what has happened."

"It is the usual story which we have heard from so many other and thought could never happen to us."

He stopped speaking because the champagne had arrived.

Lord Shield raised his glass.

"To the future," he toasted, "and may it be very much better than the past!"

"I will certainly drink to that," the Earl said, "but quite frankly for me it is impossible."

"That is a word I very much dislike," Lord Shield remarked, "but pray continue with your story."

"It is, I am afraid, such a familiar and dull story. My father felt incapable of coping with the estate and let it fall into rack and ruin."

He paused for a moment.

"He was ill for quite a few years before he died, the servants he trusted left him and the rest pilfered everything while the house fell to pieces."

He took a deep sip of his champagne.

"The debts piled up one on top of another and what I am facing now is an enormous number of bills which cannot be met. I have nothing to sell and have not the slightest idea how I can pay them."

Lord Shield sighed,

"I wish I could help you, Michael, but as you well know I have been walking a tightrope for very much the same reason as you. All I can offer you would hardly feed a rat for a week, let alone horses and cattle or anything else you possess."

"They are very likely to starve anyway," the Earl said dejectedly. "Only this morning before I came to London, the man who supplies the oats for the horses and the other foodstuffs required on the farm has refused to deliver anything more until I pay his bill."

"Have you nothing you could sell?"

The Earl gave a sharp laugh with no humour in it.

"You do not suppose that I have not thought of that? The house is in a terrible state of disrepair. It is of course entailed, just the same as the pictures, the furniture and everything else."

He gave another mirthless laugh before adding,

"Entailed for the son I can never afford to have."

"It is the most dismal story I have ever heard," Lord Shield exclaimed and poured more champagne into the Earl's glass.

"There is nothing I can do unless you can produce a good idea."

Lord Shield sat back in his chair.

He was a good-looking young man, very English and aristocratic in his appearance. At the same time there was a look of intelligence about him which was more appropriate to a scholar or a statesman than a young soldier.

The same might have been said of the Earl except that he was unusually handsome.

When he first appeared at social gatherings he had been welcomed effusively by mothers with *debutante* daughters. Now, since he had left the Army, he had found no time for such social occasions.

He had just struggled on despairingly to repair the damage that had accumulated on his estate. When he had looked at the acres of unsown land and at the farm buildings which needed urgent repair, he had felt increasingly helpless.

He had found it a Herculean task which no sensible man would have attempted in the first place.

So he had travelled to London today to call on his Solicitors. They had made it very clear to him that he was completely and absolutely bankrupt.

As if he had followed his friend's thoughts, Lord

Shield said unexpectedly,

"There must be something you can do!"

"Tell me what, John, to be truthful I might easily be sent to prison."

Again there was silence.

"I have a vague idea coming to me," Lord Shield said, "and there is just an off-chance that it might be of some help."

His voice did not sound very encouraging, but the Earl answered,

"I will try anything! I have lain awake night after night hoping for a miracle, but miracles never happen in real life."

"What I am thinking about is just that."

"Tell me about your idea."

"I read in the newspaper yesterday that a friend of my father's, who I know was also a friend of your father, has just arrived in England from America. I do not know whether you remember him, but his name is Randon.

The Earl wrinkled his brow.

"Randon?" he repeated. "No, I cannot say I remember him."

"Well, he was a close friend of our fathers a long time ago. I was just leaving Eton at the time and I remember he tipped me a fiver."

"That is certainly something to remember," the Earl agreed. "I only wish he had done the same for me!"

"Well, he knew your father and as he is presently in London, why should you not renew his acquaintance?"

"Why do you think he would help me?"

"It said in the newspaper that he is enormously rich and made his money in property in the United States."

"Do you really think I could ask his help? I should think if he has any sense at all, he would show me the door. If he is as rich as you say he is, there will be a great number of old friends holding out empty hands."

"I have indeed thought of that, and quite frankly, Michael, I was considering whether I should approach him myself, but your need appears to be greater than mine."

"Perhaps we should go hand in hand with a begging bowl," the Earl suggested, with a note of sarcasm in his voice.

"No, be serious," if he has returned to London after a long time away, he may not have many friends here and might be quite pleased to see us."

"I think it would be wise to arrive separately," the Earl cautioned, "and as you heard of him before I did, you should be the first."

"Your need, I understand, is very urgent," Lord Shield answered, "therefore you have a go first. Honestly Michael, I am not as desperate as you are."

"You can be thankful for that small mercy at any rate. I am seriously thinking of putting a bullet through my head, or just disappearing abroad where no one can find me and leaving the house to fall down and the estate to become a complete wilderness which it nearly is already."

"Of course you cannot do that."

"If your rich friend cannot help me then what am I to do? As it is, I cannot face the pensioners knowing how little money I give them and that is all borrowed from the bank."

The Earl gave a very deep sigh before continuing,

"The Church needs repair, the schools are closed because my father did not pay the teachers and I am in arrears with the wages of the few people who are still working for me."

As he spoke his voice was dull with despair.

Lord Shield threw out his arms in an almost theatrical gesture.

"Then you will have to make Randon cough up," he urged. "Remind him of the past and of your father's fondness for him. Beg him, if necessary on your knees, to give you a helping hand and if he is as rich as they seem to think he is, he will not miss a few thousands."

There was silence before the Earl admitted,

"I would rather face a whole tribe of hostile natives than have to beg for charity."

"I feel exactly the same," his friend agreed, "but if you are drowning, it is no use being particular as to who throws you a lifeline."

The Earl gave a deep sigh.

"Where is this man Randon staying?"

"At *Claridge's Hotel.*"

"All right I will go to see him and when I come back with my tail between my legs, you can show me the way to the Debtors prison!"

"I shall be hoping and praying that you will succeed, old boy, but I admit rich men are proverbially mean."

"A crust of bread is better than no bread at all," the Earl reasoned. "I will accept anything, even a fiver like the one he gave you when you were going back to Eton."

He looked at the clock on the mantelpiece.

"I will go to *Claridge's* now. I may catch him before he goes out to luncheon. If he refuses to help me, I shall look to you, John, to give me the last meal I will be able to take in a civilised place."

"If you are going, Michael – *get on with it*! As I said at the beginning of our conversation, it is just an off-chance. But sometimes an outsider passes the winning post first!"

"And more often he falls at the first fence."

The Earl rose from his chair and put his hand on his friend's shoulder.

"Thank you for the champagne, my dear John. It has given me Dutch courage and I am most grateful."

He walked away before Lord Shield could reply.

Outside the Club his chaise, in which he had driven up from the country, was waiting.

The chaise itself was somewhat dilapidated and needed repainting. However the horse drawing it was a good-looking animal and he certainly looked better fed than his owner.

As the Earl climbed into the driving seat, he was aware that the groom who handed him the reins was looking pale and thin and his coat needed repairing.

"I have another call to make, Jim, and then I will try to find you something to eat, as I expect you are hungry."

"That's nothing new, my Lord," the groom answered. "But I'll be mighty glad of anything you can give me."

The Earl did not reply, but turned the horse round and drove into Piccadilly and up Berkeley Street into Berkeley Square.

He remembered as he passed through the square that his grandfather had owned a house here. His father had sold it as soon as he came into the title.

It took him only a few minutes more to reach *Claridge's*.

The Earl made enquiries at the hotel's reception desk and was told that Mr. Randon was in his suite. He gave his name and asked if Mr. Randon would see him and a page was sent hurrying up the broad staircase to the first floor.

While the Earl was waiting, ladies and gentlemen were arriving for luncheon and a band was playing in the foyer.

It was a long time since he had lunched or dined in any expensive hotel nor for that matter in the company of people who were well off.

Several pretty women, very smartly dressed, passed the Earl as he stood with his back to the fireplace. Because he was so handsome, they first looked at him with interest and then they looked again with what was almost an invitation in their eyes.

The Earl wondered a little bitterly what they would say if they knew that his pockets were empty.

If he was to ask a lady to have luncheon with him, she would have to pay for the meal.

There were however, he noticed, several rather smart gentlemen waiting for them. They sprang to their feet eagerly when the ladies appeared.

It was a long time, he thought, since he had taken a woman out for a meal or even had the pleasure of her company.

He remembered the women he had met in Cairo when he had spent a short leave in that exotic city.

How entrancing they had been!

There was one in particular whom he had almost forgotten until now.

As he was thinking back into the past, a voice startled him,

"Mr. Randon will see you now, my Lord."

The Earl had been so far away in his thoughts that he came back to reality with a jerk.

"Thank you," he said to the page and followed him up the stairs.

As he would have expected of a rich man, the suite which Mr. Randon was occupying was one of the largest and most prestigious in the hotel.

As the Earl was ushered into the sitting room he thought for a moment it was empty.

Then he noticed that the man he had come to see was on the sofa by the window. He was lying back against silk cushions and his legs were covered with a rug.

The page closed the door behind him.

As he walked across the room he saw that Mr. Randon was a man with grey hair and a lined face.

He looked extremely ill.

As the Earl reached him he held out his hand saying,

"I remember your father well, and of course, Michael, you have grown a great deal since I last saw you when you were only a little boy."

There was a chair beside the sofa and the Earl sat down.

"I am sorry to hear you are ill."

"I am very ill," Mr. Randon replied. "But tell me about your father and when he died. I remember hearing about his death when I was in the wilds of America and could not even send a wreath for his funeral."

The Earl told him the date of his father's death, which had been over two years ago, and how he had suffered for years before he finally passed away.

"I am so sorry. Very sorry indeed," Mr. Randon said. "And what have you been doing since I last saw you?"

The Earl explained how he had taken a commission in the Army after he left Oxford and how he had resigned his commission when his father died.

He told him how he had been trying ever since to repair the damage that had been done to his neglected estate.

"I do remember your house very well."

"I would not like you to see it now, sir," the Earl replied. "Nothing had been done to it during my father's illness and the roof is falling in and very soon it will be almost uninhabitable."

"A sad story! A very sad story," Mr. Randon commented. And what are you doing about it?"

"To be honest there is nothing I can do. I have tried. I really have tried desperately, but there is too much to be done."

He paused a moment and then resumed,

"You may not know, having been abroad, but we have suffered a succession of bad harvests which have been fatal for a great many farmers."

"And your stables?" Mr. Randon questioned. "I remember well the excellent horses your father owned."

"I have three left now. Two are getting old, but there is one which I can still ride and drive, behind which I came to London today."

There was an uncomfortable silence.

The Earl knew that Mr. Randon was looking at him critically. There was no need for him to plead for help after what he had just said.

Mr. Randon who was a shrewd and clever man was obviously aware of the situation.

"What made you come to see me?" he asked.

He broke a silence which the Earl felt was almost unbearable.

"I have just come from White's," he replied, "where I was talking to my friend John, who is now Lord Shield. I think you knew his father even better than you knew mine."

"Yes, of course," Mr. Randon agreed. "Shield was a great friend of mine."

"John told me that he had read about your arrival in the newspaper and I have therefore come to see you because you knew my father."

"And because you need my money?"

The Earl felt uncomfortable and ashamed of begging from a man who was a stranger to him.

He wanted to rise and leave.

It was only by controlling himself that he managed to answer,

"It may seem a presumption, sir, but being desperate I came to see you, because of your past friendship with my father."

"How desperate?" Mr. Randon asked sharply.

Again the Earl drew in his breath.

He felt he had never been so humiliated in his whole life.

"At a rough estimate," he replied, "I owe thirty thousand pounds and have no possible means of paying it. As you will understand, the house and estate are entailed and anything saleable has already been disposed of."

"What do you think it would cost to put the whole place in working order as I remember it?"

The Earl spread out his hands.

"It would cost so much, sir, that I would not even like to guess at what would be required."

"I have not made my fortune," Mr. Randon said in a hard voice, "without being business-like. You should learn, young man, to give a straight answer to a straight question."

The Earl knew he had been rebuked.

He drew in his breath and declared,

"Very well! I should say at the least, fifty thousand pounds."

There was silence.

The Earl was convinced from the hard expression on

Mr. Randon's lined face that he would say there was nothing he could do.

He wished he could rise to his feet and shake Mr. Randon by the hand and then he could leave with some dignity before he was told to go away.

He thought Mr. Randon was merely thinking of a way to break it to him gently that he was asking too much.

Then the older man said slowly,

"I have a proposition to make to you."

The Earl felt his spirits lift.

"Proposition, sir?"

"Yes," Mr. Randon replied, "and because I have a very short time to live, I want an answer *now*."

"I understand."

"I appreciate your predicament," Mr. Randon continued, "and I am prepared to make over to you the sum you require to restore your estate and pay off your debts on condition that you marry my daughter immediately."

The Earl drew in his breath.

"M-marry your d-daughter?" he stammered, thinking his voice did not sound like his own.

"I will arrange for the marriage to take place tomorrow morning. After which you will take her away to Cariston Hall because I will be leaving England."

"Leaving England?" the Earl repeated.

He thought as he spoke that he was sounding extremely stupid.

But he was finding it hard to take in exactly what Mr. Randon was saying to him.

"I have been told," Mr. Randon continued, "by my doctors that I may die at any moment. I have developed a dislike of funerals with people weeping and wailing and I have no wish for anyone to mourn me.

"I shall therefore leave England the moment you have married my daughter, if you agree to do so and no one will ever hear of me again."

"But, sir – " the Earl began in astonishment.

Mr. Randon put up his hand.

"I have told you that your answer needs to be a direct yes or no. The funds you require, which shall we say is *one hundred thousand pounds* to make it a round figure will be paid into your bank immediately the wedding has taken place.

"As you are well aware, you will then take on the handling of my daughter's fortune, which is a very considerable one and is likely to increase as the years go by."

"But, sir, your daughter has not met me," the Earl protested. "She may – "

"My daughter will do as she is told," Mr. Randon interrupted. "I do not intend to discuss this matter any further. I am merely asking for your answer to my proposition."

The Earl felt his head was whirling and it was difficult to think straight.

How could he refuse *one hundred thousand pounds*?

How could he refuse not only to restore his house, but to help all his dependents on his estate, who had been suffering ever since his father died?

Mr. Randon was looking at him expectantly.

The Earl knew he was waiting.

He heard a voice that did not sound like his own,

"Of course, sir, I can only accept your proposition most gratefully."

"Then it is settled. I will organise everything and you

will be married to my daughter Kristina at St. George's Church, Hanover Square, tomorrow morning at eleven o'clock. I suppose you will be bringing your best man with you. He can act as one witness and I will arrange for one other. There will be no one else present."

"You mean that I shall not have the pleasure of meeting – your daughter – before I – marry her?" the Earl managed to ask.

"I am tired and have no wish to answer any further questions. Everything will be arranged and you can deal with my Solicitor as soon as your marriage has taken place."

As he finished speaking Mr. Randon held out his hand.

There was nothing the Earl could do but take it.

"Thank you!

"Thank you very much indeed, sir. I am very grateful and I can only hope – "

"Goodbye!" Mr. Randon interrupted him. "As I have a great deal to do, you will understand that I now wish you to leave."

The Earl rose, bowed and walked towards the door.

As he reached it Mr. Randon picked up a bell that was lying on a table by the sofa and rang it.

Another door opened, which the Earl thought led to a bedroom. A man who looked like a valet appeared.

As he walked towards the staircase he thought that what he just heard must be a figment of his imagination.

'It could *not* be real! How is it possible that I could be married tomorrow to a woman I have never seen and about whom I know absolutely nothing? And how could I receive one hundred thousand pounds for doing so?

'I must be mad! It cannot be true,' he told himself.

Then as he reached the hall and knew that his chaise was waiting outside, he remembered that Jim was hungry.

'I must find him something to eat,' he thought.

At the same time he knew that John Shield was waiting for him at White's.

Quite suddenly he realised that he could not return to White's.

He could not discuss with John what had just happened, as his friend who would mull over the story and find it not only unbelievable but rather discreditable.

The Earl walked out of *Claridge's*.

He stepped into his chaise and as he took the reins he said,

"I will find you something to eat, Jim. Unless it has been closed down, there used to be a good Public House at the corner of Mount Street."

He saw the groom's eyes lighten at the thought of food.

Without saying any more the Earl drove quickly through Grosvenor Square and into Mount Street.

He had not been wrong. The Public House was still there and looked as if it was doing well.

"Go inside," the Earl told him, "and buy whatever food they have ready and two bottles of beer."

As he spoke he drew a few silver coins out of his pocket and gave them to his groom.

They were, in fact, almost the last assets he possessed.

Yet, if what he had just heard was true, tomorrow he would be a very rich man indeed.

A rich man, but tied by matrimony to a woman he had never seen and who had never seen him!

A woman from whom it would be impossible for him to escape for the rest of his life.

Jim was not long in coming back carrying the beer and food wrapped up roughly in paper.

"They says, my Lord, they expects people to stay inside to eat their food, but I tells them your Lordship cannot leave the horses."

"We will eat in the Park," the Earl replied, feeling that he was in considerable need of some fresh air.

The streets, like his impending marriage, seemed to be closing in on him.

He drove into Hyde Park and stopped where there was a quiet place shaded with trees by the Serpentine. He climbed down from the chaise, taking one bottle of beer and a little of the food that Jim had brought.

He walked away to where there was an empty seat under a tree overlooking the water.

As he ate, he found himself thinking that if Mr. Randon was as ill as he said he was, he might die in the night and then everything the old man had planned would be upset.

When he went to St. George's Church tomorrow morning he would find there was no bride. No one would be waiting there except perhaps a passer-by kneeling in prayer.

'The whole situation is far too fantastic,' he thought.

Yet, like a drowning man clutching onto a rope, he wanted to believe it was true. That his home and the estate would be saved.

He had known that if the title was to carry on as it had for six hundred years, passing from father to son, he would, sooner or later, need to be married.

He had indeed been under some pressure when he was twenty and twenty-one.

He had then decided that he would not marry until he was older and fell really in love. Of course there had been women in his life. He had been far too good-looking to escape from them.

It was they who had done the hunting. Not he.

17

It would be untrue to say that he had not enjoyed them all. But it would be equally true to say that none of them had meant anything very much to him.

His mother who had died when he was twelve had been incredibly beautiful, as well as a very gentle and loving parent.

At her death he had felt as if the whole world had come to an end and nothing would ever be the same without her.

When he realised that he had to go on living without her love, he had found it a very difficult and for several years had been desperately unhappy.

It was something he could never talk about to anyone so he had repressed his sorrow within himself.

As he grew older he knew that what he wanted in a woman was the softness, the sweetness and the love he had received from his mother. Without expressing his feelings in words, he had thought that one day he would find someone like her.

She would love him, he would love her, they would be married and live happily ever after.

It had never crossed his mind when he was so hard up that he should look for an heiress, nor that he should marry a woman only because she could give him the money he so desperately required for his estate.

He had seen the fortune-hunters, because they had been all too evident, when he had gone to balls and parties in London. And there were always a great number of young girls who were known to have wealthy fathers.

But like most masculine men, the Earl had thought that nothing could be more humiliating than to be dependent on his wife, and to be obliged to ask her to pay for everything he required not only for himself but for those who were dependent upon him.

Yet now that was just what he was being forced to do.

He shrank with revulsion from the whole idea.

He appreciated that Mr. Randon had promised him one hundred thousand pounds to pay his debts, but it was really a bribe to make sure that he would fulfil his part of the contract and marry his daughter.

'I hate the whole idea,' the Earl thought, looking out over the Serpentine. Once again he felt he could hear his mother's sweet voice telling him how much she loved him.

He could feel the softness of her arms around him.

Doubtless Mr. Randon's daughter would be as hard as he was himself.

If she resembled her father, she would certainly be no beauty.

'I cannot do it!' the Earl screamed at himself.

But he knew he was deceiving himself. He had to do it because there was no alternative.

It was not only for himself. It was for the sake of his people. For the farmers who had tears in their eyes as they told him that their crops had failed and that they had lost their cows, their sheep, their pigs and even their chickens.

What they needed was money. Just as he needed money for the house and the servants who were asking for their wages. And for the pensioners who could not manage on what little he had been able to give them these last few months.

He wanted money too for the children and all those who had worked for the family for years. Like young Jim. They were hungry because he could not pay them their wages to buy food.

'I have to do it! *I must!*' the Earl told himself.

He realised that he had eaten the food Jim had bought at the Public House and drunk the beer without even tasting it.

Now he needed to find a room for the night where they would not ask him to pay in advance. There would be no point in driving back to the country and immediately having to return if he was to be at the Church on time.

He could think of various friends whom he had known in the past and if they could they would willingly provide him with a bed for the night. But they would undoubtedly ask questions as to why he was in London.

He might have to tell them why he had to be at St. George's Church at eleven o'clock tomorrow morning.

'There must be somewhere I can stay,' he pondered.

Yet it had been too long a time since he had seen any of his friends.

Then he had an idea.

He would go to the barracks of his Regiment to see the Colonel and ask if it was possible that he could stay there just for the night.

He was quite sure that he would be willing to oblige him.

He thought with a wry twist to his lips, he would spend his last night as a bachelor with the men with whom he had fought. He would be with men who were concerned with training how to fight an enemy.

They did not have to sell themselves on the altar of matrimony.

He rose from the seat by the Serpentine and walked back to his chaise. Jim was licking his fingers as if he did not wish to waste a crumb of the food he had bought for him.

He had obviously enjoyed every mouthful. The Earl thought he would arrange, without too much difficulty, for Jim also to spend the night at the barracks.

'My last night of freedom,' he whispered to himself, 'and God knows if it will be a night I shall always remember.'

CHAPTER TWO

The Colonel of the Regiment was delighted to see the Earl, who had known him only slightly when he had been in the Army and he found an old comrade-in-arms, Captain Charles Stuart, who took the Earl into the Officers' Mess.

There were a number of young Officers whom the Earl had not met and just two whom he had known in the last year before he had resigned his commission.

They all welcomed him in a most friendly manner and when he sat down to dinner with them he was enjoying every moment.

Half way through the meal Captain Charles told him that he and three other Officers were going to a party at Lady G's and he must come with them.

"Lady G?" the Earl queried, "who is that?"

"She is always known simply as Lady G," Captain Charles explained. "You do not know who she is?"

"I have no idea."

He was then told that Lady G was quite a famous personage on the London scene. She had been a beauty in her time and had married several husbands.

The last one had an unpronounceable Greek name.

When he died he left her a large amount of money but, as she said herself, when she was too old to enjoy it. She

21

therefore gave parties at which she welcomed any number of gentlemen.

She saw to it that they were amused by young and attractive women.

"Most of them are married," Captain Charles explained, "or say they are. Quite frankly, Michael, your mother would not accept them, but they are all very pretty and the greatest fun."

"It sounds something new and original," the Earl agreed. "There was certainly no Lady G in my day."

"We get the best champagne free and you will see for yourself tonight what a joy it is, especially for young Subalterns with no friends in London."

The Earl became curious.

At the same time it prevented him thinking about what was lying ahead of him tomorrow.

He was trying not to remember that this was his last day of freedom.

Yet it kept recurring to his mind that he should enjoy himself while he still had the chance.

He also learned that his friend Charles Stuart was leaving the following evening for India. He had been appointed to a post at Viceregal Lodge in Calcutta and was looking forward to his new posting enormously.

"Equally I shall miss being at home," Captain Charles commented. "However much I travel and I know you will say the same, there is nowhere like one's own country."

"I agree with you," the Earl answered. "But if you are not leaving until the evening Charles, there is something I would like you to do for me at eleven o'clock tomorrow morning, if you would be so kind."

"Of course," he replied, "I will do anything you want."

"I will tell you about it later, and thank you for saying

that you will help me in a matter of great importance to me."

He had worried as to whether he should ask John Shield to be his best man, but with Charles going away the same evening, it would make it easier for his marriage to be kept a secret.

The dinner in the Officers' Mess was excellent and because he felt he needed it, the Earl had a great deal to drink.

Then the five of them set off when dinner was finished to Lady G's house in Chelsea, which was an impressive mansion standing in its own garden.

When they arrived they found they were by no means the first.

There were quite a number of young men present already, besides what the Earl noticed to be some extremely pretty women.

Lady G, who was well over sixty, came towards Charles with open arms.

"I am so glad to see you, my dear boy," she cried. "I was worried in case you were prevented from coming tonight. I would then have asked too many women, which would be a disaster."

"I would still have you, Lady G," Charles replied enthusiastically, "and you are more important than all the rest."

"Now you are flattering me, you naughty boy," she burbled slapping him gently on the cheek.

"I bought a friend of mine," Charles continued. "We served together in the Army before he became the Earl of Cariston."

Lady G held out both her hands.

"I knew your father many years ago, and he was as handsome then as you are now."

It was just possible, the Earl thought, to realise that she had been beautiful when she was younger. Now she was lined and had lost her figure, but she certainly made the best of herself.

She was glittering with jewels.

Her hair, which was obviously a wig, was well arranged and she was dressed in a most expensive and fantastic gown.

"Now come and have something to drink," Lady G invited the Earl. "Charles will have told you that I boast a cellar which is the envy of London and I am sure you are a connoisseur when it comes to wine."

The Earl thought with a smile of amusement that he had not been accused of that particular vice before.

He did however appreciate the excellence of the different wines he was being offered, but he thought it best to stick to the very good and extremely expensive vintage champagne.

Lady G was chattering away to him and at the same time she obviously was looking round the room for someone she wanted him to meet.

Finally she a made a small sound of satisfaction as a beautiful young woman came walking towards her.

She had dark hair, eyes that flashed like diamonds and a dazzling white skin.

"I was hoping you would come tonight, Rosie," she trumpeted as the woman kissed her. "Let me introduce you to a charming young man whose father used to be as handsome as he is. Lord Cariston – Lady Rosemary Wheldon."

Lady Rosemary gave the Earl a dazzling smile.

When he took her hand he was aware that she wore a wedding-ring, beside one set with diamonds.

"Come and dance," she suggested. "I have been sitting all day and I need the exercise."

The Earl glanced at Lady G to see if it was rude to leave her. Then he realised she had already turned away to welcome some newcomers.

Lady Rosemary led him into what appeared to be a small ballroom, which was lavishly decorated with flowers. There was a small band playing on a platform at one end.

There were only two other couples dancing.

When the Earl put his arm around Lady Rosemary's small waist, he realised that she was a very good dancer if a somewhat intimate one.

She certainly clung to him very closely.

As their steps seemed to match each other's, he recognised that he was lucky enough to have found a really excellent partner.

"Tell me about yourself," Lady Rosemary asked in a soft caressing voice.

It was a tone the Earl had often heard before. It was the way women invariably spoke to him almost as soon as they met.

"I am only a country Squire," the Earl replied, "and the reason we have not met before is that I have not been in London for a very long time."

"Well, now you have come back, we must make it impossible for you to leave," Lady Rosemary cooed in her entrancing voice.

They danced for some time and then walked into another room where small tables were romantically lit with pink candles. Without asking wine was immediately placed in front of them.

Looking into his eyes, Lady Rosemary drank his health.

"Have you come here alone?" the Earl enquired, "or is there someone waiting impatiently to claim you for the next dance?"

"I want to dance with you," she purred. "If one comes to Lady G's, it is always a mistake to bring anyone with you who may be inclined to be possessive."

The Earl could not fail to understand her implication so he escorted her back to the ballroom for another dance.

Later he found there seemed to be no one else at the party except Rosie, as she told him to call her.

No one interrupted them or even asked if they were enjoying themselves. They were alone in the world in which they danced, drank and danced again.

Finally, because it was so hot in the ballroom, Rosie suggested they should move into the garden.

They walked slowly over a smooth lawn until under the trees the Earl saw that there was a summer house. The door was open and there were just a few candles lighting it.

He could not remember afterwards if he had found it by chance or whether Rosie had guided him there.

Out of curiosity he looked inside and found it contained a large comfortable looking divan on which a number of soft cushions were arranged.

"Shall we sit here?" he suggested.

As he was speaking Rosie closed the door.

Then her arms were round his neck and it was impossible to think of anything else.

*

It was one o'clock in the morning when the Earl heard Charles Stuart saying,

"I have been wondering where you were, Michael. We should to be getting back to the barracks."

The Earl opened his eyes.

He had been asleep on the comfortable divan and there was no sign of Rosie.

He pulled himself up and Charles helped him into his coat which he could not remember taking off.

"It has been a jolly good evening," Charles said conversationally. "But I expect you are tired, after coming up from the country this morning."

"Yes, indeed I am."

He put on his shoes and walked across the lawn beside Charles.

"Lady G has gone to bed," Charles informed him, "so there is no need for us to say goodbye to anyone, although I expect some of the party will go on dancing until dawn."

The Earl was forcing himself to return to reality. He sensed that it was somehow remiss of him not to say goodbye to his hostess.

And for that matter to Rosie.

However it was easier in the circumstances to leave as Charles had suggested and there were only the two of them being driven back to the barracks.

The Earl thought it was tactful not to enquire what had happened to the other Officers who had come with them.

"What I am asking you to do tomorrow morning, Charles," he began as they drove away, "is to be the best man at my wedding."

Charles looked at him in surprise.

"At your wedding? I always remember you saying you had no intention of getting married until you were much older. Who is the fortunate young lady?"

"I do not want to talk about it. I just want you to do me the great favour by being my best man at what is to be a secret marriage."

The Earl paused before continuing,

"The wedding is to take place at St. George's, Hanover Square at eleven o'clock this morning. It will not be announced in the newspapers and I do not want anyone to find out that it has happened for a long time."

"It all sounds most mysterious. Are you in any particular trouble, Michael?"

The Earl guessed that Charles thought he was being blackmailed into marriage perhaps with someone he had seduced.

"No, no it is not that," he replied quickly. "It is a hurried wedding because the bride's father is extremely ill, and I have no wish for anyone to talk about it until it can be properly announced at a later date."

"I understand and of course I promise you, Michael, I will tell no one if that is what you want."

"Thank you, Charles, I know I can rely on you."

They drove on in silence until they reached the barracks.

Then as they climbed upstairs to the bedrooms, the Earl asked,

"Please tell someone to call me fairly early otherwise I might easily oversleep."

"I will see to it," Charles promised.

The Earl walked to his room. He had brought enough clothes to London to stay for one night.

He had intended to dine at White's before everything had happened in such an extraordinary way, and he had therefore packed his dinner jacket which he was now wearing.

He was relieved to see that while he had been away one of the Regimental batmen had pressed the clothes he was wearing when he arrived.

They were not particularly smart, but he thought they would have to do, whether the bride liked it or not.

Once in bed he realised he was still sleepy and if he was honest he was still suffering slightly from too much champagne.

At the same time he could not help thinking a little cynically that he had just spent his last bachelor party in what might be described as 'style'.

He wondered if he would ever see Lady Rosemary again.

She had certainly lifted him for a moment with a flame of passion that most men would find irresistible.

'I should be grateful to her,' the Earl thought.

However he really had no wish to see her again.

It took him a little time to fall asleep.

The menace of what was going to happen so soon was beginning to prey on his mind.

*

The Earl awoke at six o'clock when the troops were roused and the whole barracks seemed to come alive like a beehive, so he closed his eyes and tried to return to his dreamless sleep.

However sleep was impossible and he could only think of what lay ahead of him.

How should he respond to the wife who had been thrust upon him?

If, as he expected, she looked in the least like her father, – plain, overbearing and extremely authoritative, he was going to find life very difficult.

He had always disliked what he considered to be pushy, aggressive women who thought they knew better than men and, where possible, tried to rule the roost.

He could not imagine a worse fate than being married to one or having to fight for authority in his own house.

Yet the Hall would no longer really be his.

How could it be, when she would have paid for the food that was put into his mouth?

For the servants who waited on them.

For every repair, and Heaven knows there were enough repairs needed at Cariston Hall to employ a regiment.

'I should be grateful for what John guessed was just the chance of a miracle,' the Earl kept telling himself.

Equally he could not help feeling his whole being revolt at what he was being forced to do.

A batman called him at eight o'clock and informed him that breakfast was being served in the Officers' Mess.

"Captain Charles has had to go out, my Lord," the batman informed him, "but he says he'll be back at ten o'clock."

"Thank you," the Earl replied, "and will you please tell my groom that I require my chaise at ten thirty precisely."

He had a quick bath and dressed himself, trying to look as neat and smart as he could, although his clothes were well worn and somewhat threadbare.

Definitely not smart enough for a bridegroom of his standing, but there was nothing more he could do.

Except, he thought sourly, that it was only what the bride would expect the pauper she was marrying to look like.

He wondered if perhaps she would be as reluctant as he was to marry someone she had never met.

Then he told himself cynically that like all young women she was out to snare a title, which was in fact all she would gain from this marriage.

He was very conscious of the fact that, because he was

an Earl and the seventh member of his family to hold the title, he was a matrimonial catch.

Not a very impressive one, but still a catch.

He could doubtless have pursued an heiress himself as many of the aristocratic friends had done and he might even have found one who was attractive.

She might then have coincided a little with the perfect wife he had dreamed he would find one day.

Actually he would never have done so because he would have thought it too humiliating.

Now he was in an even more degrading position.

His bride had been chosen for him and he had never seen her and she would doubtless dislike him as much as he already disliked her.

All these thoughts and a great deal more flashed through his mind as he was dressing.

He forced himself to appear at ease as he walked downstairs for breakfast.

There were quite a number of Officers still in the Mess, including the Colonel.

"Did you enjoy yourself last night?" he asked. "I hear they took you to Lady G's and that invariably means a night of too much drink and too many pretty women!"

The Colonel laughed and the Earl managed to laugh too.

"That describes it exactly, sir."

"Well we are very lucky to have found the old woman," the Colonel continued. "She is certainly a unique institution in London and they tell me there is no one like her in any other capital city in Europe."

He drank a sip of coffee before he added,

"You know I mean that it is all for free and what young Subaltern, who is invariably penniless, could ask for more?"

"I do agree with you," the Earl replied.

He wondered vaguely if Rosie was thinking of him this morning or perhaps after she had crept away when he was asleep, she had never given him another thought.

She was certainly very pretty and he had been lucky that she had taken his mind off himself at least for the hours they had been together.

"I suppose you are travelling back to the country today," the Colonel was saying.

"Yes, I think so."

The Earl wondered as he spoke if his bride would think it a poor sort of honeymoon.

She would certainly find no comforts at Cariston Hall and it was doubtful whether there would be much to eat for dinner.

He supposed he ought to do something about it, but somehow he felt limp and it was too much of an effort to try to think ahead.

All he kept remembering was that he was due at St. George's in Hanover Square by eleven o'clock.

There he would be married.

At the same time he would receive an enormous cheque which would change his life completely from the moment it was in his possession.

He looked around the table at the Colonel and the other senior Officers and conjectured at what they would say if he told them what he was about to undertake.

He supposed most of them would think he was very lucky and the others would undoubtedly despise him for selling himself, or rather his title, for that was what it really amounted to.

Now he thought it over, he felt certain that, if he were just Mr. Nobody, the wealthy Mr. Randon would have behaved differently.

He might have given him a small amount for the sake of '*Auld Lang Syne*' and would then have looked elsewhere for a son-in-law higher up the social tree.

Of course *that* was the answer and he was very stupid not to have realised it earlier.

As the Earl of Cariston, he had something concrete to offer and Mr. Randon had been well aware of it.

He wanted an aristocratic husband for his daughter and who better at a moment's notice than himself?

An Earl with a long family history behind him, he was also the son of a man who had been Mr. Randon's friend in the past.

'This is what has happened,' the Earl told himself, 'and I need not feel as humble as all that!'

He mused that what it actually meant was that he need not be subservient or under any obligation to his wife simply because she could pay for anything he required.

By the time breakfast was over the Earl felt he could still carry his head high.

Even though he was selling himself at the altar.

Charles appeared promptly at ten o'clock to say he had been making last minute preparations to leave for India as the P&O liner on which he was sailing would leave Tilbury just before midnight.

"Will you be back for luncheon?" the Colonel enquired of him.

"Yes, sir," Charles answered. "I have an engagement this morning and after that I shall be free."

"I would like to have a last few words with you," the Colonel said, "so do not forget. I expect however, you will have a large number of people to say goodbye to."

He walked away without waiting for an answer.

Charles turned to the Earl,

"Not as many as all that. My family, as you know, live in Derbyshire and I have already said goodbye to them. But there was a very pretty girl I met last night and I have every intention of saying farewell to her when you have finished with me."

"I do not think I shall be keeping you very long," the Earl replied dejectedly.

Jim, who looked as if he had enjoyed himself, brought the chaise round to the Officers' quarters.

The two men climbed into the front with Jim behind.

There seemed nothing particular to say, so they did not talk as the Earl drove down Birdcage Walk and into Green Park.

The sun was shining and it was obviously going to be a warm and pleasant day.

Charles was looking around him as if he was taking a last glimpse of London before he travelled to India.

The Earl could remember doing the same when he had first gone abroad.

When he was in the Sudan he had felt extremely homesick at times and often thought that people at home forgot how monotonous service life could be in a foreign country.

A soldier usually could not even speak the language and, when he was not actually campaigning, there was very little to do.

He had been fortunate in that he always enjoyed reading and had managed by hook or by crook to find books wherever he was posted.

The majority of his brother Officers in their time off just smoked and drank and longed for a pretty girl to talk to.

There was no Club for them like White's or Boodles,

where they would always find other friends with whom they had been at school or university.

"How long do you expect to be in India?" the Earl asked as he drove across Grosvenor Square.

"I suppose three years at least," Charles replied. "It will be exciting to see it all, but I shall miss the family and of course being with the Regiment."

He laughed and added,

"In fact I feel as if I was going to a new school and was the youngest and stupidest boy in the class!"

"I know exactly what you are feeling, but cheer up, Charles, I hear that the Viceroy lives in great grandeur and the women in Simla are very attractive."

"That is what I have heard," Charles answered, "but I will believe it when I see it."

They reached Hanover Square and the Earl could see St.George's Church looming ahead of him.

As he drew up his horse outside he confided,

"I am very grateful to you for doing this for me Charles and please remember not a word to the Colonel or anyone else."

"You can trust me and the best of luck, old man."

Charles spoke with sincerity.

The Earl could only hope that what he was wishing could come true.

He handed the reins to Jim and walked up the steps and through the great portico into the Church. He had been here before, but he had forgotten how large and imposing it seemed, especially when it was empty.

Then as he looked ahead at the altar he saw to his surprise that someone had already arrived.

He was not late, in fact it was just ten minutes before eleven o'clock.

As he walked up the aisle he saw an elderly man with white hair and beside him stood a young woman.

If she was the Bride, she was smaller than he had expected. She was wearing a pale blue dress and on her head what seemed to be a bonnet trimmed with blue flowers.

As he drew nearer the Earl saw that a veil covered her face, which prevented him from seeing her at all clearly.

When he reached the altar, the man came forward to hold out his hand.

"I think you must be Lord Cariston," he said, "and the Vicar said that he would start the service the moment you arrived."

The Earl turned towards his future wife, but she was apparently unaware of him as her head was bent.

He would have spoken to her, but at that moment the Vicar wearing his surplice appeared from the Vestry.

He stood on the steps in front of the altar and the bride with the elderly man immediately walked towards him.

There was nothing the Earl could do but follow them as he had been told to do and the Vicar started the Service.

He intoned the words of the marriage service clearly and sincerely.

The Earl considered that under the circumstances he would have thought that the wedding was very well conducted and in fact quite moving.

Yet because of the woman standing beside him, the Earl could feel resentment rising in his breast and it was with the greatest difficulty that he forced himself to attend to what the Vicar was saying.

When it came to the point where the bride was given away, the elderly man did so.

Next the ring had to be blessed and the Earl, with a start of horror, realised he had done nothing about providing one. It had simply not occurred to him.

He wondered what he could do.

But he noticed that the man escorting the bride was giving something to Charles.

A moment later a ring was placed in his hand.

He realised that it was exceedingly remiss of him not to have remembered it but he had to admit Mr. Randon had thought of every last detail.

The Vicar blessed the ring and turned to the Earl,

"Repeat after me – '*with this ring I thee wed*'."

Obediently the Earl repeated the words.

As he placed the ring on the bride's finger, he noticed that she was trembling and the responses she gave were in such a soft unsteady voice that he could hardly hear them.

'So she *is* frightened,' he thought.

Yet just as he was horrified at what was happening to both of them, there was nothing he could do about it.

They knelt for the Blessing.

When they rose they followed the Vicar as would be usual into the Vestry to sign the Register.

It was laid out for them on a table and the Earl signed first. Just as the bride took up the pen, the man who had come with her said,

"I must have a few words with you, my Lord, and I have arranged with the Vicar that we can do so here."

He moved to the other end of the Vestry table and as the Earl followed him, he realised that the Vicar was taking the woman who was now his wife back into the Chancel.

It was then that Charles spoke up,

"I do not think you will need me any longer, Michael. If you will forgive me, I still have a great deal to do before I leave."

"Of course, Charles," the Earl replied, "and the very best of luck to you. I am sure you will enjoy India enormously and so many thanks for your help today."

"I only wish you were coming with me," Charles sighed.

They shook hands and Charles departed.

The Earl closed the door behind him and turned to face the elderly man.

"I think I should introduce myself, My Lord," he began. "I am Ernest Trenchard, Senior Partner of Trenchard, Moreton and Pollit, Solicitors to Mr. David Randon."

It was rather as the Earl had expected, so he did not say anything as he sat down in a chair at the end of the table.

"First of all," Mr. Trenchard announced, "I have instructions to give your Lordship this."

As he spoke he handed him a cheque for ninety-nine thousand pounds. The Earl looked at it in surprise and Mr. Trenchard resumed,

"I also have here one thousand pounds in cash, which Mr. Randon thought you might need whilst you are travelling back to the country."

The Earl still did not say anything.

However his lips tightened as he thought that while Mr. Randon was entirely right in his conjecture, it was slightly insulting that he should demonstrate in such a fashion his awareness that he was in fact penniless.

"I think it would be wise for me to suggest," Mr. Trenchard was saying, "that this cheque together with the other documents I would ask you to sign should be sent by courier this afternoon to your Solicitors wherever they may be."

"They are in Oxford," the Earl informed him, "which is, as you may know, about ten miles from my house."

"I thought that was likely," Mr. Trenchard commented.

The Earl told him the name of his Solicitors and he appeared to have heard of them.

Then he produced a paper on which Mr. Randon had given him Power of Attorney over all his wife's possessions and anything she should inherit in the future.

The Earl did not even look to see how much was involved, although he was quite certain that it was an enormous sum almost beyond his imagination.

He just signed wherever Mr. Trenchard asked him and also gave a specimen of his signature to be kept by the Solicitors in London.

"I am sending the documents by a courier who is waiting outside the Church," Mr. Trenchard said briskly. "He should reach your Solicitors before they close this afternoon."

"Thank you, I am sure you have thought of everything and I am most grateful."

He did not sound particularly grateful and Mr. Trenchard added,

"If you are in any difficulties, my Lord, just get in touch with me and I will do everything in my power to assist you."

"Thank you very much," the Earl replied.

"Of course," Mr. Trenchard continued, hesitating slightly, "as we have been Solicitors to Mr. Randon for over twenty years, it might make matters easier if you saw your way, my Lord, to appointing us as your own Solicitors. But that of course is a decision only you can make."

The Earl stiffened.

"I will think about it," he said, "and thank you for arranging for these documents to be conveyed to my Solicitors in Oxford. But I would like the cheque paid directly into my bank in Oxford."

As he spoke he wrote down the name of his bank and its address. As he did so he thought that at least the money would be entirely under his control and out of the hands of Mr. Randon's Solicitors.

He could not quite understand why they should wish to control his affairs as they already controlled the affairs of the man who had just become his father-in-Law and of course his wife.

Again he sensed that it was an attempt to take away his independence. And he was fighting for every inch of the way.

As if Mr. Trenchard sensed that it was a mistake to say anymore, he merely bowed.

"I will see to it that this cheque is delivered to your bank at the same time as the documents go to your Solicitors."

"Thank you again," the Earl replied and walked towards the door.

As he went back into the Church, he saw that his bride was kneeling in front of the altar and the Vicar was standing by her as if he was still blessing her.

When he appeared Kristina rose to her feet.

The Earl approached the Vicar and said,

"I must thank you very much for taking the service."

"It was a pleasure, my Lord," the Vicar answered. "And as I understand it you do not wish your marriage to be talked about at the moment, so I can assure you that nothing will be said by anyone here."

The Earl nodded.

He wondered if he should offer his arm to his wife to walk down the aisle. However she had already started to walk ahead and he could only follow her with Mr. Trenchard at his side.

Outside the Earl found a large chaise drawn by four horses and to his surprise there was no sign of Jim.

Before he could ask any questions Mr. Trenchard told him,

"On Mr. Randon's instructions, your man was told to return to the country. This chaise and the four horses are a wedding present to you and he thought you would wish to drive them to Cariston Hall."

For a moment the Earl could not think what to say so Mr. Trenchard continued,

"Luncheon has already been ordered for you at the *Crown and Anchor* on the Oxford Road, which you should reach in about two hours."

The Earl was speechless.

Everything was being arranged for him so that he felt he was a puppet being manipulated by the hands of an expert showman.

With a superhuman effort he held out his hand to Mr. Trenchard saying,

"Thank you very much. I do appreciate all that has been done for me."

Whilst he was speaking, his wife had stepped into the chaise and when he walked round to the other side to take the reins, he saw that the groom in charge was a middle-aged man, who looked as if he was well experienced with horses.

The Earl took the reins from the groom who climbed into the back seat and they started off.

The Earl did not wave to Mr. Trenchard, but he did however notice that his wife sitting beside him had raised her hand.

The Earl could not help being annoyed at the way he had been treated like a child.

His own horses and groom had been sent away without consulting him, yet he was forced to admit that the four horses he was driving were perfectly matched and an outstanding team. They were admired by almost everyone they passed in the streets.

It was the sort of team he had dreamed of, but never thought he would possess.

He was also very conscious that the comfortably padded and well-sprung chaise was something he could never have afforded.

Because the Earl was an excellent driver he managed to weave the horses quickly through the traffic.

They reached the outskirts of London in what he recognised was record time. The horses were obviously fresh and as the Earl gave them their heads he thought it would be impossible anywhere to find a finer team which now incredibly belonged to him.

His wife sitting beside him had not spoken since they left the Church.

He wondered what she was thinking about.

It suddenly occurred to him that she would not expect, being so rich, to travel without a lady's maid.

He supposed that if Mr. Randon had arranged everything else, he would have sent a maid ahead to look after her when they arrived.

Again he could not help feeling he should have been consulted – even so he had to be fair and admit it would have been impossible for Mr. Randon to have done so.

The reason was quite simple – he would have had no idea where he was.

'I must be grateful for everything I am receiving and try not to resent it,' the Earl admonished himself but he knew he was going to find it difficult.

He was vividly conscious of the woman sitting beside him.

She had not said anything nor had she even looked at him, as far as he knew, from behind her veil.

He thought it rather strange that she should have been married in blue and he noted that she had worn her veil right over her face as if she did not wish him to see her face.

As a bride her face should have been covered and it would have been his privilege to raise the veil when they had reached the Vestry.

Of course at some weddings it was the practice to kiss the bride.

The Earl drew in his breath.

He did not want to think about it.

It would be best for him to concentrate on the splendid horses.

They drove on and as there was little traffic outside London, the Earl was delighted with the speed they were maintaining.

He only wished that John or one of his other friends could be with him as they would appreciate this outstanding team.

Because he felt he must say something to his bride, he drew in his reins a little and with a great effort remarked to her,

"These are the finest horses I have ever driven. Have you or your father had them long?"

For a moment there was silence.

Then in a voice he could hardly hear she replied,

"No, I – have never – seen them – before."

CHAPTER THREE

The Earl thought that it was a strange answer to his question.

He was however busy turning a corner so he did not say any more.

They drove on in silence until he found that they were close to the *Crown and Anchor* where Mr. Randon had arranged their luncheon.

The Earl drove into the courtyard of the inn and ostlers came running to take the horses' heads as the groom jumped down from his seat.

Knowing that the horses would be well looked after, the Earl walked round to help his wife out of the chaise to find that she had already alighted.

"This is where we are taking luncheon," the Earl announced, thinking he must say something. He supposed that she must know already as she did not reply. She merely walked ahead of him into the hostelry.

The proprietor was waiting to receive them with so much bowing and scraping that the Earl understood he was very impressed by their arrival.

While he was talking to the proprietor he saw a maid in a mob cap escorting his wife up the stairs.

"A private room has been arranged for your Lordship,"

the proprietor informed him, "if you'll please come this way."

He walked ahead down the passage and opened a door. The private room was small but comfortable and there was a table laid for two.

There was also, the Earl noticed, a bottle of champagne on ice and he accepted a glass which the proprietor poured out for him.

He wanted to ask questions as to how everything had been organised and who had done it, but thought it would be a mistake.

The proprietor, having handed him a menu left the room.

When the Earl looked at what had been provided for their luncheon, he sensed that it had been chosen with great care. It was definitely a luncheon far beyond the usual meal that could be obtained in a country inn.

He thought that one thing about his new father-in-law was that if he did anything he did it well. No one could appreciate more than he did the team of horses he had been driving.

He finished his glass of champagne.

He was wondering why his bride was taking so long to join him when the maid in the mob cap entered the room.

She bobbed a curtsy before she said,

"Her Ladyship's compliments, my Lord, and as she's feelin' tired she hopes you'll excuse her not coming down to luncheon. She's havin' a little soup in her room and will be ready to continue the journey when your Lordship sends for her."

The maid gave her message in a hurried, breathless voice as if she was afraid she might forget what she had been told to say.

"Will you tell her Ladyship that I completely understand," the Earl answered, "and I hope she will feel better for the rest."

The maid bobbed another curtsy and departed.

He sat down with a sense of relief as at least he would not have to talk during the meal and the sooner they reached Cariston Hall the better.

When the food arrived it was excellent and he enjoyed his luncheon and the wine that was served to him.

When he had finished he called to the waiter,

"Please bring my bill and ask someone to tell her Ladyship I am ready to proceed on our way."

The waiter left the room.

A few minutes later the proprietor appeared.

"There's no bill, my Lord. Everything was accounted for when your Lordship's luncheon was ordered."

"Who gave the orders?" the Earl enquired.

The proprietor hesitated.

"A man, I think, my Lord, he was a senior servant, ordered the luncheon and paid for it on your Lordship's behalf. I hopes it were to your satisfaction?"

"It was indeed excellent."

The Earl was curious who the servant could be and he gained the impression that the proprietor knew little more than he did.

He tipped the waiter generously and then walked to the courtyard where the groom had already turned the horses round and was looking as if he too had enjoyed a good meal.

The Earl climbed into the driving-seat wondering how long his wife would be.

Perhaps she was going to be one of those women who was late for every appointment. If so it was something he would find very annoying in the future.

However it was only two or three minutes later when Kristina appeared. She came hurrying through the door still wearing her hat with the veil and sprang lightly into the seat beside him.

The Earl wondered if, in fact, she had not been as tired as she had said, but merely wished to avoid having a meal alone with him.

But he dismissed the thought as it was most unlikely that a young girl would feel that way for most women were only too delighted to be in his company at a meal whether it was a good or bad one.

He drove off realising that there was only another two hours to go before he would reach Cariston Hall.

He had left early yesterday morning in despair and now he was returning in triumph, driving horses that he never imagined in his wildest dream he could afford to own.

It did occur to him that now he could replenish his stables and perhaps in the not too distant future he would be able to go to Tattersall's sale rooms to buy some really outstanding horses.

Then he scolded himself severely.

There was a great deal to do first with his newly acquired wealth before he could think of indulging his own pleasures.

A Herculean task was waiting for him at the Hall and it would require time, effort and thought as well as money to set all matters right.

As he drove on he was thinking that the farmers must come first. He would repair their buildings and see that they had all the livestock they required. They would need new ploughs and new farm machinery for their fields.

He was deep in thought.

They had nearly reached Cariston Hall before he

realised he had completely ignored his wife sitting beside him. She had not said a word since they had left the *Crown and Anchor*.

Trying to make his voice sound as pleasant as possible the Earl informed her,

"We are nearly home and I do hope that when you see it you will admire my house."

He paused for a moment before continuing,

"I expect your father will have told you that the Hall is in a very bad state of repair. There is a great deal to be done to it as well as to the estate all of which will certainly keep me extremely busy."

There was no reply.

He glanced at his wife wondering if perhaps she had gone to sleep but she was however sitting upright looking straight ahead.

Although he could not see her face because of the veil, he was sure she was wide awake.

"The Hall," he continued, "actually goes back as far as the sixteenth century when the original house was built by the second Earl of Cariston. I have some prints of it which you might find interesting, but of course it has been altered and added to over the centuries. My grandfather spent a great deal of money putting on a new front at the beginning of the century."

He finished speaking and waited for a reply and at last it came.

In a voice he could hardly hear, his wife replied hesitatingly,

"It – sounds v-very – i-interesting."

The Earl felt he had done his best and could do no more.

Maybe she was feeling ill or she was disliking the

situation in which they found themselves as much as he did.

All he could think about was the sooner they arrived at the Hall the better and if she wanted to rest, there were plenty of empty rooms available.

Finally the Earl turned in at the iron gates which were always open because there was no longer a lodge keeper.

As he did so he felt with a sigh of relief that at least he was home. If nothing else there would be everything that was familiar to welcome him.

He drove up the long drive.

The grass on each side needed cutting and was thick with fallen leaves and branches from the ancient oaks. Ahead he saw the lake, the bridge over it in need of repair and then the Hall itself.

It was still beautiful despite the fact that a large number of windowpanes were cracked and the roof over the East wing had fallen in.

The Earl drew up the horses outside the impressive front door.

He notice that the front door was open and there was a man standing just inside and he wondered who it could be.

It was most likely to be someone from the estate, who would have come as soon as he appeared to complain of more damage or more likely an unpaid bill.

The groom sitting behind the Earl jumped down and came to his side to take the reins.

"The stables are through the arch over there on the left," the Earl told him. "I am afraid you will find conditions are rather difficult, but my groom, Jim, who came on ahead of us, will be able to help you find proper accommodation for this excellent team."

"I am glad your Lordship is pleased with them," the man said respectfully.

"Very pleased indeed."

As he finished the conversation he found his wife had stepped out of the chaise without help and was waiting for him at the bottom of the steps.

"I think we have made the journey in record time," he said as he joined her. "Now let me show you my house."

When he reached the top of the steps, he saw what appeared to be a smart butler bowing respectfully to him at the open door.

"Welcome home, my Lord," the man said, "and may I have the privilege of wishing your Lordship and Ladyship every happiness."

"Thank you very much, now will you tell me who you are?"

"My name is Brook, my Lord," the man answered, "and Mr. Randon sent me and my wife here, thinking you might find us useful."

"You have worked for Mr. Randon?"

"For seven years, my Lord. We have been travelling with him in America, but when he left England this morning in his yacht he had no further use for us."

"Then I shall be very glad to employ you at Cariston Hall."

"We will do our best to serve your Lordship in the same way we have served Mr. Randon," Brook continued. "My wife's an excellent cook, although of course she's always had help in the kitchen."

"As I expect you have already found, the only people in the house at the moment are a very old couple, the Hunts, who have been looking after me because they have nowhere else to go."

There was a hard note in the Earl's voice as he spoke as he had been forced to dismiss all the other servants.

The old couple had begged that they might stay even if he did not pay them, as they were too old to find other employment and might be forced into the workhouse.

They had therefore stayed on doing what they could, preparing his scanty meals and making his bed for him.

The Earl recognised at once when he looked at Brook that he was a competent man.

"We also brought with us, my Lord," Brook was saying, "an elderly maid who was prepared to leave *Claridge's* so as to attend to her Ladyship."

"I am glad to hear that, and later I will talk to you about the household requirements and decide what additional staff we will need."

He thought as he was talking to Brook that he should by rights be consulting his wife.

So he turned to speak to her only to find that she was already half-way up the stairs accompanied by an elderly woman who he imagined was the lady's maid Brook had been talking about.

He thought it a little surprising that she had walked away without saying anything to him.

"I took the liberty, my Lord," Brook said, "of putting a bottle of champagne on ice in what, I think, must be your Lordship's study. Perhaps you would like a glass after such a long journey?"

"Thank you very much, Brook, that is an excellent idea."

The Earl thought that matters were certainly different from what he had expected on his arrival.

At the same time he could not help feeling a slight resentment. Mr. Randon had organised everything without taking him into his confidence and he would have liked to have expressed his own wishes regarding the new arrangements in his own house.

He was however only too aware of what a mess the place was in. It had been impossible for the old couple, Hunt and his wife, even to clean out the fireplaces and during the winter he had just thrown a log or two onto the ashes.

The floors were obviously unbrushed and all the furniture undusted.

The Earl walked into his study and did not fail to feel ashamed at the torn and worn leather covers on the chairs and the curtains were almost in shreds.

There was however, as Brook had said, a bottle of champagne waiting for him in a silver ice-bucket that was emblazoned with his crest.

It was a valuable piece of silver which fortunately – although it had seemed at the time unfortunately – had been unsaleable as like the rest of the silver it was entailed.

Brook poured out the Earl a glass of champagne and handed it to him on a silver salver which he noticed had been beautifully cleaned.

As he took the glass the Earl said to Brook,

"Having seen the house and the dilapidated state it is in are you and your wife prepared to stay with me? You know without my saying so that I need servants and a large number of them, to clean the house and restore it to what one might call working order."

He thought as he spoke that Brook was doubtless aware without being told that the servants could now be paid and why the house was in such a desperate need of repair.

"We're not only prepared to stay, my Lord, if you'll have us," Brook replied, "but I'd like to take on the responsibility of running the establishment off your Lordship's hands. It is what I always did for Mr. Randon, who was far too concerned with his business to have time, after his wife died, to engage servants or to see that they performed their duties properly."

The Earl paused for a moment.

He realised that in a way that he would be sacrificing his authority and that it should really be his wife's job to run the house.

Yet as Brook and his wife had been with her father she would no doubt be content to allow him to put the house into proper order.

The Earl stood with his back to the empty fireplace and thought carefully before he responded,

"What I want to do is to employ as many people as possible from the villages that I own. There are five of them, the largest one being at our gates."

"In that case, my Lord, I am sure it'll be easy to find the housemaids we require, women for the kitchen, and the footmen who I am prepared to train."

"That would certainly be a load off my shoulders, and I am sure that her Ladyship will be agreeable, as I am, to you taking charge."

Brook bowed.

"I will do my best to give your Lordship every satisfaction and I'll make enquiries immediately as to who is available locally."

"Thank you very much, Brook."

"If Your Lordship will excuse me, I will go and see if her Ladyship requires tea. Will your Lordship prefer tea in here?"

"This is the only room I have been using," the Earl answered. "I shut up the drawing room some time ago, as you have doubtless already discovered."

He had in fact shut all the other reception rooms, as it depressed him to see the dust covers over the furniture with all the curtains drawn and to know the dust was accumulating day by day and there was no one to do anything about it.

He slept in the master bedroom where his father and his ancestors had always slept.

Downstairs he only used the study and the dining room and as it was a very large room, he would not have eaten there if there had been an alternative nearer to the kitchen.

Unless he had eaten in the servants hall, it was the nearest for Hunt, who had rheumatism in his legs, to carry the food his had wife cooked.

The Earl thought now he could open all the rooms with footmen in the hall as there had always been when he was a boy.

He could employ a number of housemaids and a housekeeper, who would rustle round the bedrooms seeing that everything was spotless.

In the past the windows had shone like jewels in the sun and he could remember big log fires warming every room in the winter.

An elderly servant's duty had been to keep all the fires burning. He had gone round the house putting a fresh log on each fire every half hour.

'I can hardly believe this can all happen again,' the Earl sighed to himself.

Tomorrow he could take a message of joy to the farmers who had been so despondent.

If Brook was filling the house with servants, he must not forget the gardens. His mother would have wept if she could see the overgrown flowerbeds and the unmown lawns. Weeds had crushed what was left of the flowers in the herbaceous borders.

'Who could have better luck than I have?' the Earl asked himself again.

Then he remembered the source of his luck and that she was upstairs.

He felt a little shiver surge through him.

It was so intense that he poured himself another glass of champagne, although he knew it was unnecessary to drink any more when he was just about to have tea.

Brook brought tea into the room a few minutes later. He had found a tea-table which the Earl's mother had always used and a lace tablecloth to go over it.

"I must apologise, my Lord," Brook said in his usual respectful voice, "that I have not yet had time to clean all the silver. Your Lordship has some very fine pieces of early Georgian, if I may say so, but it'll take me a little time to make them look as they should."

"I am afraid everything has been very much neglected, so engage all the help you can, although I think you will find it hard to find anyone locally who is experienced."

"I shall be able to manage, my Lord," Brook said confidently. "However I am afraid there's very little to eat for tea and your Lordship will have to wait for dinner."

"It is my fault," the Earl confessed, "I should have thought of buying something on the way and of course you had no one to send to the village."

"I brought with me what my wife planned to cook for your Lordship's dinner," Brook replied, "but I must admit I forgot that her Ladyship would require tea and that your Lordship might have enjoyed a hot scone or a slice of fruit cake."

The Earl laughed.

"I have not had such delicacies for a very long time. I cannot even remember what they taste like!"

"Things will be different tomorrow, my Lord."

He looked at what he had placed on the table

disparagingly before adding,

"I will inform her Ladyship that tea is served."

Brook left the room and the Earl walked towards the window and outside he could see the garden overgrown with weeds, remembering how different it had looked years ago before his mother died.

Then he heard the door behind him opening and thought it must be his wife.

He turned round but it was Brook who entered the room.

"Her Ladyship's compliments, my Lord, and she hopes your Lordship will understand that she doesn't feel well enough to join your Lordship at tea or for dinner."

"I understand," the Earl answered, "and of course her Ladyship must rest until she feels better. I suppose she has everything she requires."

"The woman we brought down with us, my Lord, whose name is Martha, will find her everything that's available, and tomorrow it will *all* be different."

"Thank you, Brook."

When Brook had withdrawn he looked at the tea. He saw there were some small sandwiches and a plate of biscuits.

He could understand that Brook thought there should be cakes and scones and many other delicacies to complete a proper English tea.

That was what Mr. Randon must have enjoyed all the time he was in America. Brook would doubtless have forced the Yankees to accept English ways even when they ventured out in the wilds or wherever Mr. Randon journeyed in his search for money.

Then as if he could not keep still, the Earl strode out of the house and into the garden.

He had been more concerned during the past few years with the agricultural parts of the estate and had therefore forgotten that not only was the flower garden a disgrace but so was the kitchen garden – all three acres of it.

It was just a riot of weeds and the glass in the greenhouses was broken and the flowers, peaches and grapes were all dead.

He walked round, calculating how quickly he could put back the clock. He wanted to make everything look exactly as it had been when he was a boy.

Now he could not see a square yard of soil that did not requie attention so he decided that he would need six or more gardeners even to begin the task of clearing and replanting.

'I can do it,' he thought, 'but first I must look after the farmers. I will see to them first thing tomorrow morning.'

He would have liked to jump on the one horse that was left in the stables and ride round this evening.

Then he had to consider two points.

First that the horse in question had brought Jim back from London and it could obviously not be taken out again.

Secondly that he now had a wife. Although she apparently had no wish to eat with him, he felt he would have to see her sometime this evening.

'She is your wife,' a voice seemed to say inside his brain. 'Although she is tired she will doubtless expect you to behave on your wedding night as a bridegroom should.'

He shrank away from the thought but it persisted in his mind.

When he returned to the house he wondered if it would be polite to go to her room and ask her how she felt – at least if she felt too ill to see him she could say so.

She had managed to avoid having luncheon and tea with him and had now declined dinner.

He remembered how quickly she had managed to spring in and out of the chaise and how she had hurried up the stairs as soon as they had arrived.

He did not believe that she was feeling ill. In fact he suspected that she felt a revulsion, as he had, at being married.

She was therefore avoiding her bridegroom as long as it was possible to do so.

If so, it was a new experience for him as he had never met a woman who tried to avoid him, nor had he known one who had not sought every opportunity possible of sharing his company.

'Whatever it is, at least I am free for the moment,' the Earl thought as he headed for the stables.

He wanted to see if the new team that he had driven down from London were settled and cared for.

He found the groom in charge had certainly seen to their comfort, as there was fresh hay in each of their stalls and food which must have come from London was in the mangers. And although the buckets were dilapidated, the water was fresh.

There was accommodation for a number of grooms at the end of the stables in a building which had been built a hundred years ago.

The Earl thought he should go and find out if the new groom was properly accommodated.

When he drew near, he could hear him and Jim talking and laughing and as they were obviously quite content, he thought it would be a mistake to interrupt them.

'I will talk to them tomorrow,' he decided, 'and if I am to buy more horses, I shall require more grooms and they will be perhaps easier to find than the staff Brook needs in the house.'

He walked back to the house as the light was fading and now he must go upstairs to change for dinner.

It was something he never did when he was alone.

He had always been too tired and the dinner, which consisted usually of one course, was hardly worthy of the name.

Now he recognised that Brook would expect him to behave like a gentleman as he walked upstairs to his room.

He was not mistaken.

His clothes had been laid out for him and there was a bath set down in front of the fireplace and there was a large brass can of hot water standing beside the bath and another containing cold water.

The Earl smiled to himself.

This was indeed luxury.

As he sat in the bath he only hoped that Mr. Randon could appreciate how much he appreciated the difference he had made to his life.

When he had dressed himself in his evening clothes, he wondered once again if he should knock on his wife's door.

She was in the next room which had once belonged to his mother. He had meant, if he had been asked, to put her somewhere else.

The Earl thought it must have been Brook who had insisted she should occupy the Countess's room.

The Hunts, on his instructions, would have unlocked the door and done what they could to dust and tidy the room.

Actually because it belonged to his mother, the Earl had taken more care of that room than any other.

When he had been alone and fighting desperately a losing battle against his debts he had often gone into her room on his way to bed.

He could almost see his mother sitting in her favourite armchair.

When he was small she would smile and hold out her arms and he would run towards her and sit on her lap. He told her everything he had been doing. What he had learned from his governess or where he had been with his nanny.

Everything she had said to him and the love in her eyes and in her voice, he could never forget, but he now hated the thought of anyone else using her room.

It never struck him for one moment that the Countess's room was where his wife was expected to sleep, or that the servants would instinctively take her there.

'She will spoil it,' he told himself.

He wanted to turn her out and make her choose any of the other bedrooms in the house, but not that one.

'Perhaps I will be able to move her tomorrow,' he mused as he walked past the room and down the stairs.

At the same time he was angry.

Once again he had not been consulted and everything was happening too fast for him.

'I *will* be Master in my own house,' he told himself, 'and I will not permit any interference from the servants nor from my wife.'

He walked to his study to find that Brook had lit the fire, which made the room feel cosy and took away the slight feeling of damp.

The walls were dry at the moment, but during the winter some of the external bricks had cracked and they all needed repointing.

Now the fire made the room feel inviting and the setting sun was shining through the window.

"Dinner is served, my Lord," Brook announced from the doorway.

The Earl strode alone into the dining room.

It was very much as he had left it two days ago except that the table had been polished and the four silver candlesticks had been cleaned.

When dinner arrived the Earl realised that Mrs. Brook was an excellent cook.

Although the food must have come down from London, every dish tasted fresh and delicious and was totally different from anything that the Earl had eaten in this room for a long time.

Brook served him wine which he knew had not come from his own cellar, which was practically empty.

When the Earl had finished, he said,

"Will you thank your wife for an excellent dinner and see that she has every possible help she requires in the kitchen."

"Very good, my Lord. But Mrs. Hunt has been very helpful tonight and I know your Lordship will be pleased to know that we are getting on well with the old couple."

The Earl retired to his study.

He sat down in the chair beside the fire with a writing-pad in his hands and started to make a list of the calls he must make tomorrow morning.

It was important he should go first to the farmer who had been on the estate the longest.

He was also making notes of what he would promise to provide for them immediately and he could imagine their joy and delight after so many years of misery.

For the first time in what seemed years he could visit them eagerly as lately he had been reluctant to listen helplessly to their endless complaints and despair.

He completed a long list of what he must do.

Then Brook came in to ask if there was anything

further he needed and bade him goodnight.

The Earl thanked him once again.

"It has been a pleasure, my Lord, and I am looking forward to seeing Cariston Hall looking as fine as in the past."

Then because he had had very little sleep last night and the night before, he felt his eyes closing.

In fact he must have dozed for a little while.

When he roused himself with a start, he realised that the fire had sunk low and had almost gone out.

'I must go to bed,' he thought.

Then he remembered his wife.

However late it might be, out of sheer good manners if she was not asleep, he must ask her if she was comfortable and if there was anything he could do for her.

He placed his notes on the writing table, blew out the oil lamp by which he had been working and he walked towards the door.

Brook had left a lamp burning in the hall and the Earl could see its light at the end of the passage.

He wondered if later he might be able to afford to install gas or perhaps even the new electric light which everyone was talking about it since it had been seen in one of the theatres in London.

Personally the Earl missed the silver sconces which had held the candles, but they burned down very quickly and candles were more expensive than the small amount of oil which was necessary for the lamps.

The Earl walked along the passage and decided he would pick up the lamp and take it with him upstairs.

As he entered the hall he saw to his surprise there was someone at the front door reaching up towards the bolt and it took him only a second to realise that it was a woman.

She was having trouble as she was too short to reach the bolt. Even standing on tiptoe she could only just touch it with her fingers.

The Earl stared at her back and then became aware of who she was.

When he reached her, as if she had not heard him approach, she screamed and moved to one side.

"Why do you want to open the door?" the Earl asked.

She did not answer but shrank even further away from him, turning her head as if she did not want him to see her face.

"Where are thinking of going, Kristina?"

"A-away," she replied stammering over the word.

"Where to?"

There was silence until he said,

"I think if you are running away you should tell me where you are going."

"To – the – Convent," Kristina replied.

The Earl was astonished.

"The Convent?"

"I – want – to – go. Please – let me – go."

Now her voice was pleading as she looked up at him.

By the light of the lamp which the Earl carried in his hand he could see her face for the first time.

He thought he must be dreaming.

She was not in the least what he had expected, which was a hard-faced, plain woman who resembled her father.

Instead he was looking at what seemed to be no more than a child.

Very large blue eyes were looking up at him with an expression of fear he had never seen in any woman's face.

They seemed to completely dominate her small nose,

her pointed chin and the golden hair which curled on her oval forehead.

She might, the Earl thought, have been a child of no more than ten or twelve years old.

She was looking at him like a little girl who was terrified of being punished for something she had done.

"If you want to run away," he said after a moment, speaking very quietly, "it is impossible for you to do so in the middle of the night, unless you have someone meeting you."

It suddenly struck him that perhaps that was the reason why she was so reluctant to have anything to do with him.

She was in love with someone else.

"It – is not – that. It – is just that I – have to go back to the – Convent. I want – to be – a nun."

The words seemed to tumble out of her perfectly shaped lips.

The Earl stared at her in amazement.

"A nun!" he exclaimed. "But that is impossible!"

"Perhaps they will just let me stay for a while," she replied.

Her words were almost inaudible.

"I think," the Earl said quietly, "we should talk about this and we can hardly stand here in the hall doing so. Let us go into my study and you can tell me why you want to run away. I promise I will listen to everything you have to say."

"I thought – as it was so quiet," Kristina said almost beneath her breath, "that – you were – asleep."

"I admit I was for a short time, but it was in a chair and not in my bed. Come along, Kristina, let us go into the study."

He put out his hand as if to help her.

She shrank from him in a way which made it quite clear that she was terrified of him.

The Earl started to walk ahead, hoping she would follow him. He found it difficult to understand what was happening or why she felt as she did.

He thought now that he should have talked to her on the journey down from London.

As he reached the study he found she was just behind him.

When he walked into the room he lit the lamp on his desk and threw two logs of wood onto the fire.

The bottle of champagne that Brook had opened for him was still there, so he poured a little into two glasses and walked back to Kristina.

She had not sat down as he expected but was standing by a chair looking at the fire.

"I think," he ventured, "you have been deprived of the champagne which was provided for us on our wedding day."

He saw her give a little shiver and her hand holding the glass was trembling.

"Please sit down, Kristina. Do not be frightened, but tell me why you are so upset and why you want to go to the Convent."

He spoke in a very gentle, quiet voice.

He had found in his varied life that it was often effective with men who had committed some crime or women on the verge of hysterics.

For a moment he thought that Kristina was going to refuse him.

Then she moved very slowly forward to sit down on the end of the armchair.

CHAPTER FOUR

The Earl moved to sit down in a chair next to Kristina.

Then he noticed that her hand was trembling so much that the champagne in her glass was spilling over, so he picked up a small table from the other side of the fireplace and put it down beside her.

He was aware as he did so that she moved backwards as if she was afraid he might touch her.

He also saw that the light from the lamp on the writing-table was behind him, so he picked out a spill from the vase on the mantelpiece and held it down to the flames just beginning to leap in the fireplace and lit two candles.

Now he could see Kristina far more clearly and noted that she was wearing a cape over her shoulders and a hood covered the back of her hair.

She placed the glass of champagne which she had not touched on the table beside her.

"I think," the Earl suggested, "you will find it quite warm by the fire, so I should take off your cape."

She did so, undoing it at the neck and letting it slip down beside her.

He realised that the only luggage she had been carrying was a handbag.

As he sat down in the chair he said in a quiet and what

he hoped was a reassuring voice,

"Now that we are comfortable, I hope you will tell me exactly why you are running away. After all as I am now your husband it *does* concern me."

He saw the colour come into her cheeks.

In the light of the candles he thought she was even lovelier than when he had seen first her at the front door.

She did not answer and after a moment he continued,

"You were going away apparently without any luggage or any conveyance waiting for you outside. How did you intend to travel to the Convent, wherever it may be?"

She did not speak and he thought he was not going to receive an answer.

Then at last in a hesitating, frightened little voice she said,

"The convent is – in Florence.

"Florence!" the Earl exclaimed. "How on earth could you have travelled there on your own unless someone was looking after you?"

"I thought – that I would be able to find – a courier who would arrange it for me."

"I suppose because you wished to escape from me?"

Again the colour flushed into her cheeks and she looked away from him.

"Did you tell your father that you did not wish to marry me?"

"I – tried, but he did not – tell me until this morning – that was what I had to do."

"Not until this morning! Just before he left England?"

Kristina nodded.

"He said – he was going away to die – and there was

someone – who would look after me and I had to – marry him."

The words came out jerkily and the Earl could understand what a shock it had been for her.

"As I saw your father yesterday morning, he could have told you then. But perhaps he was afraid that you would run away."

"I would have done so – when he told me I was – to be married," Kristina murmured. "But I had – no money."

The Earl raised his eyebrows.

"No money?"

"Only a little – Italian money, but Mr. Trenchard when he took me – to the church, he – gave me five hundred pounds."

The Earl judged it to be a small sum considering the amount he had received.

But he supposed that Mr. Trenchard would have looked on it as pocket money for the heiress.

"So with enough money, you thought you would be able to find your way to Florence, but why should you want to go there?"

She looked at him with a faint air of surprise.

"It is where – I have been living for the last – seven years."

"Seven years! Then the Convent you are talking about is really a school?"

He knew that there were several Convents in Europe which aristocrats used as 'finishing schools' for their daughters. It was where they spent the last year before they became *debutantes*.

It was supposed to give them a Cosmopolitan polish besides a knowledge of languages that might be useful for their future.

"Now I think I understand, as you have been living at this Convent school in Florence, you thought of it in a way as home."

Kristina did not say anything but he thought she agreed.

"Surely," he resumed, "you stayed with your father for the holidays."

Kristina shook her head.

"He was very busy – in America – so after Mama died and I was sent – to the Convent, I did not see him – until I returned to London – two days ago."

The Earl felt that this was extraordinary behaviour on the part of Mr. Randon, but he did not like to say so.

As if she divined his thoughts, Kristina continued,

"Papa was – so miserable after Mama died – that he just worked and worked, and said he did not have any time for me – but I must be well educated."

"And that of course you achieved in Florence."

"I hope so, but I was – the only girl who did not seem to have a – family to – love her."

Now there was a pathetic note in her voice and the Earl asked,

"What did you do in the holidays?"

"Sometimes if the Mother Superior – endorsed them, I visited the homes of girls – who were my friends, but she was very particular as to which – invitations I could accept. I think she was frightened that – Papa would not approve."

There was another long silence until the Earl said,

"Now I can understand, Kristina, why you had no wish to be married in such a hurried manner and why you were frightened of me."

Kristina twisted her fingers together before she replied in a voice he could hardly hear,

"The nuns said – that it was very wrong and – wicked to let a man – touch me unless I loved him – with all my heart – and soul."

The Earl had no idea how he should respond.

It was something he had never thought about before and he did appreciate that it must be a terrifying and traumatic experience for a young and innocent girl to be suddenly married to a man she had never even seen before.

"I suppose," he said after a long pause, "that you understand why we were married in this strange manner."

"Papa said that as he was going – to die and could no longer look – after me, he had found someone – he trusted and whose father had been – a friend of his."

"That is true, but I think it would be fair if I told you that when I approached your father yesterday morning, he had not seen me since I was a small boy."

He thought there was a flicker of interest in Kristina's blue eyes as he continued,

"You can see that this room is in a very bad state of repair and so is the whole house. My father, who died two years ago, had been very ill for a long time while I was abroad and had neglected both the house and the estate."

He looked at Kristina to see if she was listening and saw she had turned her head towards him.

"I did my best when I returned from the Army, but there was no money and things instead of improving, grew worse. When I went to see your father I owed an enormous sum of money and I had not the slightest idea how I could pay my bills or support the people on the estate who relied on me."

"And Papa – helped you?"

"He gave me a very large sum of money on condition I married his daughter."

Kristina muffled a sound which might have been a cry.

"That was – wrong, *very wrong* – when we do not love – each other."

"That is what I thought too," the Earl agreed. "But I was at my wits end and there was nothing else I could do. I am extremely grateful to your father for saving me when I might have had to go to a debtor's prison."

He saw from the expression on Kristina's face that she was horrified at the idea.

"Now you are – safe?"

"I am safe," the Earl said, "but only if you stay with me."

"What – do you mean?" Kristina asked.

"If you run away and become a nun then I should feel obliged, if I was to behave like a gentleman, to return the money I have been given on the condition that I will look after you."

"What would – happen then?"

"The house would fall down. The farmers and all the workers on the estate would starve and I would doubtless be behind bars!"

Kristina gave a strangled murmur.

"I did – not know. I did not – understand."

"I know that. So what we have to do, Kristina, is somehow make the best of a bad job."

"You – mean," she asked hesitatingly, "that I must stay here with you – and not go back – to the Convent."

"It may seem very unpleasant to you at the moment, but for me, I am afraid there is no alternative. Quite frankly I think you are too young to decide that you wish to be a nun."

"They were always – very kind to me."

"And you really think you would want to give up your life to the Convent?" the Earl questioned. "You are young and pretty and the world can be a very exciting place if one has enough money to enjoy it."

He saw that she was looking at him with surprised eyes.

"You must realise that your father has left you a great deal of money. You can have the best horses to ride. You can give parties if you wish to. You can travel all over the world in comfort."

He smiled before he added,

"I have travelled as a soldier and although it was often extremely uncomfortable, I found it exciting."

"But you – did not have to – marry anyone to do that!"

The Earl was silent while he thought quickly.

"If you did not want to marry *me*, Kristina, quite frankly I did not want to marry *you*."

He saw her eyes open a little wider as if she had not even considered that possibility.

"You mean – you did not want – a wife?"

"I have always told my friends that I had no intention of marrying until I was very much older. It was only because I was absolutely desperate and, as you will learn, a great number of people on the estate are on the verge of destitution that I agreed to your father's suggestion."

Kristina drew in her breath.

"So you want – to be in love before – you married?"

"Of course I do," the Earl answered. "I have never asked anyone to marry me, Kristina, nor have I ever found anyone whom I wanted to take my mother's place in this house."

He had not meant to say those words but somehow they came to his lips.

"I am sorry – I never thought you would – feel this way."

"And I am sorry for you," the Earl replied.

He took a sip of his champagne.

"What I think we should do now, if we are to be sensible, is to think how we can plan the future so we are both happy and you are not frightened.

"I think the best idea would be to start at the beginning and realise that we are two strangers who have been thrown together by fate, but need to work together to save a lot of other people who are miserable and unhappy."

"You mean – that we would not really – be married?"

Because once again she was blushing, the Earl understood exactly what she was going through her mind.

"What I am going to suggest," he said, "is that we behave to each other as two ordinary people would do if they had struck a business arrangement to work together. Of course in doing so we would grow to know each other."

Kristina looked at the fire.

Then in the small frightened voice she asked,

"You – would not – touch me?"

"I promise you," the Earl replied quietly, "I will not touch you until you ask me to do so."

He was aware that Kristina gave a deep sigh because what had frightened her most was no longer such a threat.

Then as if she had reasoned the plan out for herself, she said,

"We – could just be – friends?"

"Of course, and you must understand, Kristina, that it is *your* money I shall be spending on repairing the house and restoring the estate."

She did not answer and he added with a somewhat wry smile,

"All I have to offer you is my title. It is very old and prestigious, but it has become somewhat dilapidated over the years."

"I think that was – why Papa made me marry you – he said he wanted me to marry an Englishman – whose name was respected and he would never permit me – to be snatched up by a fortune-hunter."

"I think your father was frightened that might happen and he would be too ill to protect you."

"I had no wish – to marry anyone at present – and certainly not in such a hurry."

"I felt the same," the Earl answered. "But now, Kristina, as you appreciate the situation, I suggest, as I have already said, that we start at the beginning. We have just met and first of all we need to get to know and understand each other. That will be almost as exciting and difficult as exploring a new country."

Kristina actually laughed.

It was a very pretty sound and the Earl noted that it changed the expression on her face.

She no longer looked so frightened.

"I would never have thought of myself – as a new country," she commented, "but I have often longed to explore parts of the world – that I have not yet seen."

"Perhaps one day we will be able to travel. I can assure you that there are some very lovely places to explore, although it is often a most uncomfortable journey to reach them."

"Will you buy a big yacht – like Papa's? Then we would not have to worry – about trains and ships. Actually I expected – when I was running away tonight to have to – walk to the station."

"It is two miles away and I think you would have

found it rather frightening wandering about in dark lanes all by yourself. Although you are in England, you still might find yourself in a great deal of trouble if you move about at night alone, especially carrying a handbag which looks as if it might contain valuables."

"What you are – really saying, is that I was being – very foolish. But I was so frightened – and you are so big and strong that I thought – I could never stand up to you or make you listen – to what I had to say."

It was something no woman had ever said to the Earl and it was certainly a new thought that he felt was more menacing than attractive.

"Now you know that all I want to do is to protect you from being hurt and if possible from being unhappy. So I think, Kristina, that we should start as we should have started on our wedding day by drinking each other's health."

He held up his glass which still contained a little champagne and Kristina reached out for her glass which she had not touched.

"To us both," he proclaimed. "We are pioneers setting forth on a journey of exploration to find, if we are lucky, some happiness and light."

He bent forward as he finished speaking and touched Kristina's glass with his.

Then as he drank his champagne, she took a little sip from her glass.

"That was a – lovely toast," she said, "and now I am not afraid any more."

"I think we should both retire, but you must promise me, Kristina, that you will not try to sneak away again, so that I wake up in the morning to find you gone and have to waste my valuable time looking for you."

He made it sound quite funny and Kristina gave a little laugh.

"I promise you – I shall stay here," she assured him. "But please – if you are going to meet the people on your estate to tell them that their lot is going to improve – can I come with you?"

It was something the Earl had not anticipated and just for a moment he thought she might be rather an encumbrance – it might be embarrassing to take Kristina with him.

Then he understood that she was making an effort to play her part.

There was no alternative but to accept her idea.

"Of course you must come with me and I suppose we should ride two of the horses your father gave us as a wedding present."

"I would – very much like to. I rode when I was in Florence – but we were somewhat restricted. I would love to gallop very fast – without anyone telling me not to do so!"

The Earl smiled.

"You shall gallop as fast as you wish – that is the one thing that I *can* give you freely."

As he finished speaking he rose to his feet and Kristina rose to hers.

She picked up her handbag and would have reached for her cape, but the Earl bent forward taking it from her chair.

As he did so he was aware that she moved quickly away from him as if she was afraid he might touch her. It was an instinctive movement and he sensed that while she had said she was no longer afraid, fear was still present within her.

He put the cape over his arm and blew out the candles on the mantelpiece.

As they both walked towards the door he took the lamp he had been carrying when he had found her in the hall.

As they moved along the passage side by side, the Earl thought how everything had changed and so far away from what he had been expecting.

Kristina was so small that her head only just reached his shoulders. Now he noticed that she was very slim with what was in fact a perfect figure.

However with her fair hair and blue eyes, it was difficult to think of her as a grown-up woman.

She seemed, he thought, a child who had found herself in this mess through no foolishness on her part, and was in fact suffering quite unfairly just because she was so rich.

As they started to climb the stairs he detected Kristina's glance at the front door which remained locked and bolted.

He wondered if secretly she would rather have been on her way towards the station, determined to reach Florence and find the familiarity and peace that she craved.

As if Kristina could read his thoughts, she said,

"I suspect – you are right. I should have found myself in a great deal of difficulty – and trouble all on my own."

"Forget it now," the Earl replied. "We all make mistakes, but we always hope that we will not have to pay for them eventually."

They had climbed to the top of the stairs and he walked along the corridor to open the door of her room. As he did so he said almost as if he was talking to himself,

"This was my mother's room and no one has been allowed to sleep in it since she died."

"Then I will move out – if you wish it," Kristina answered quickly. "It is a very beautiful room and although I was so frightened – I felt as if it was trying – to help me."

"If you feel like that I think you should stay here and we can talk about it tomorrow.

"Go to sleep, Kristina, and remember that tomorrow will be an adventure, something we must both try to enjoy together."

"I think – it will be – very exciting," she whispered.

She smiled at him and the Earl smiled back. Then he walked out of the door saying, "goodnight Kristina," and closed it behind him.

As he walked to his own room he felt that what had just happened was the most extraordinary experience of his whole life.

How could he have imagined for a moment that Mr. Randon would have married him not to the hard faced, plain young woman he had expected, but to a graceful, sensitive and pretty child who was obviously ignorant of the ways of the world?

She obviously knew very little about life except for her experience at the Convent school. He had expected to have to fight against an over-powering bossy woman who would continually be reminding him it was her money that he was spending!

Instead he found himself in the position of teacher and protector to a child who might almost have just emerged from her nursery.

In all his experience with women, the Earl had never had anything to do with young girls. Firstly because he thought they would bore him and secondly because he might find himself married to one.

Now incredibly that it had happened. He was married to a childlike creature to whom he would have to teach the basic facts of life apart from anything else.

How could she know anything about the struggle he had endured to run his estate, to provide for and help his people? To deal with their problems as well as his own, and if it was possible, make them happy and prosperous.

He suddenly felt very tired, but his head was still whirling with questions to which there were no answers and the feeling he was facing intractable problems to which he must find solutions.

He undressed and as he got into bed he told himself he would just have to play it by ear and hope for the best.

He had once been given command of a platoon of soldiers who were completely untrained and who had never been abroad. They were stationed in what seemed like the middle of a desert with nothing to think about except themselves.

Somehow he had knocked them into shape and he had begun to understand their feelings as well as his own. He found himself finding the development of each individual soldier of interest to him personally.

He now thought he would have to start from scratch teaching Kristina about the world in a country that she had apparently not visited for seven years and where she had no friends or relations and no one to turn to except himself.

He could understand her terror.

She had been married unwillingly to a strange man she had never seen before, who looked as she had said, big and strong and menacing!

Of course her whole situation made her want to run away.

If he had not lingered in his study, the Earl mused, she might have left after he had retired and he would not have discovered that she was missing until tomorrow.

He could see all too clearly what a panic there would have been!

If Kristina had been unlucky she might have met a highwayman, who would have robbed her of everything she possessed. Or perhaps a drunk could have assaulted her!

How could she know of the dangers that could be found in dark lanes and poverty-stricken villages?

'She is safe for the moment,' the Earl thought to himself. 'Equally I must take no risk of her trying to escape again.'

He looked back on his own life.

He could remember a number of times when he had found it wise to escape from a beautiful woman who was pursuing him. Naturally it was one in whom he had no further interest.

He could not think of one who had wanted to run away from him and certainly not one who was so defenceless that he was entirely responsible for her.

He found it hard to envisage himself as a sort of governess or teacher.

Then because the whole situation seemed so completely and absolutely ridiculous, he laughed.

*

The next morning at eight o'clock the Earl was called by Brook, who drew back the curtains to allow the sun to pour in.

The Earl was pleased that it was a fine day and exactly what he required for riding over the estate.

He then remembered that Kristina had said she wanted to come with him, but perhaps she would still be too tired.

He told himself he was being considerate in thinking that if she was wise she could stay quietly in the house to recover from the trauma of yesterday.

He would try to come back to the Hall to join her for luncheon.

Yet if he was honest with himself he knew he really wished to go alone.

"Breakfast will be ready in half-an-hour, my Lord,"

Brook said, "and I took the liberty of sending Jim to the village early this morning as there wasn't anything to eat."

"I am sorry, I should have given you some money last night. It was very remiss of me. I thought about it and then forgot."

"It is alright, my Lord. Mr. Randon tipped me very generously when I left and also gave me a sum of money to spend travelling to the Hall which was more than we needed."

The Earl thought it was very honest of Brook to say so. When he had climbed out of bed he took a number of pound notes out of the drawer.

"I want you," he said to Brook, "to go to the village and pay all my bills and of course to buy everything you and your wife require in the way of food and provisions."

He paused for a moment before adding,

"I am visiting the farms this morning, but I am afraid they will have very little with which they can provide us until they are restocked."

"I understand, my Lord, and I'll make the best arrangement I can until we gets the wheels turning as they should."

The Earl smiled.

"I am leaving the house entirely in your hands," he said. "But of course ask her Ladyship if there is anything she requires."

"Certainly, but I think your Lordship understands that her Ladyship's never been with her father since her mother died."

"I find that hard to comprehend. Surely Mr. Randon must have wanted to see his daughter."

"He was so stricken, my Lord," Brook answered, "when his wife died that all he wanted to do was to work and forget everything in his life but business. When he sent Miss Kristina to Florence, he thought he was preparing her for the life she would live in England when she grew up."

The Earl looked puzzled,

"You mean Mr. Randon was living in a somewhat rough manner?" he enquired.

"Not exactly, my Lord, he sold the house in which he'd been so happy with his wife and continually moved from hotel to hotel. Sometimes he bought a farm which he thought would interest him and at one time he owned a mansion on Fifth Avenue. But he had to keep moving and it would be impossible for any young lady to be properly educated under those circumstances.?

"I am beginning to understand," the Earl said. "It seems very hard that her Ladyship had no home to call her own and that is why we must try to make the Hall a home for her."

"It is what she has missed," Brook said.

When he left to organise breakfast, the Earl reflected that he was an extremely intelligent man and he felt himself very lucky to have someone so competent to take over the running of the house.

He knew only too well how much was required in the kitchen where the stove should have been replaced years ago and even the paved floor itself needed repairing.

Brook however would see to everything and leave him free to cope with the chaos on the estate.

When the Earl walked downstairs he found that breakfast was served in the room his father and mother had always used. Of course the Hunts must have told Brook where it was.

To his delight there were several silver dishes on the sideboard and the coffee was in his best silver pot which had been spotlessly cleaned.

The Earl was just about to help himself to eggs and bacon and what looked like some very edible sausages when Kristina came running in.

"I know I am late," she said, "but my new maid, Martha, had no idea where to find what I wanted to wear – and of course it was at the very bottom of the third trunk we opened!"

The Earl then realised that Kristina's luggage had travelled down with Brook and the lady's-maid.

He noted that her search had been successful, because she was wearing a very smart riding habit and thought with a smile it would be more appropriate in Florence than on his rough unploughed fields.

"It is so – exciting," Kristina said, as she picked up a plate, "to be going riding. I only hope the horses are rested after their long journey yesterday – and are not too tired."

"I expect if we have survived then they have too. "Of course I have three horses of my own. But two of them are old and the third also came down from London yesterday and will, I am sure, be too tired to move very quickly."

"Then we must ride on two of the team. Have you any idea when the – others will arrive?"

"What others?" the Earl enquired.

"Did Papa not tell you?"

"I do not think he mentioned horses."

"He told me," Kristina said, "that the man who used to look after his racehorses when he lived in England had bought six horses for him at Tattersall's, which he thought were outstanding – as well as the team we were driving. So I expect they will arrive sometime today."

The Earl was astonished.

"I have not heard anything about this, but of course I am delighted for many horses as possible to fill the stables.

The only thing is we shall have to do is engage some stable boys quickly to look after them, unless you are prepared to do it?"

Kristina gave him a quick glance to see if he was being serious or joking.

When she saw he was smiling she responded,

"I do not think I would make a very good stable boy – and I am sure Brook could find us some from the village. Martha was telling me as she dressed me, that they are all agog with anticipation at coming up to work at the *Big House*."

"The whole village?" the Earl asked in mocked dismay.

"I would not be surprised – the Hall is large enough for a whole army to clean it."

"If you are criticising my home," the Earl commented with mock severity, "I shall feel extremely insulted. If you only knew how I have struggled to keep this poor old house alive, you would be very sorry for me."

"Martha said that the Hunts think the world of you. They said you would share your last crust with them and that there has never been a gentleman like you!"

The Earl laughed.

"That is praise indeed. And that reminds me, I must go and see the Hunts. They were so busy helping Brook and his wife that I did not see them last night."

He finished his breakfast and strode towards the kitchen.

The Hunts were both with Mrs. Brook, who was a good-looking woman with rosy cheeks and a rather large figure as if she enjoyed her own food.

The Earl shook hands with them all and then he took the Hunts to the servant's hall to speak to them alone.

He told them how much he appreciated all they had done for him while he was struggling to keep the place going.

He gave them the wages they were owed multiplied by five times and also an extra gift of one hundred pounds to buy anything they particularly required.

Mrs. Hunt burst into tears and Hunt said,

"You've been a real gentleman to us, my Lord. My wife and I will never forget your kindness. We'd like to stay on here if you will keep us."

"You can stay as long as you live," the Earl replied. "I look on you as part of the family and could not do without you."

At his words Mrs. Hunt cried even more and Hunt shook his hand saying,

"We'll serve you, my Lord, until we die and I hopes that'll not be for a long time."

"I hope so too," the Earl agreed. "And I look to you, Hunt, to show Brook the ropes and to advise him as to who to engage from the village. We know those who would be more trouble than they are worth."

"You can leave it to me, my Lord," Hunt replied.

The Earl knew that he was delighted to be consulted and that he had been afraid of being pushed to one side because he was so old.

The Earl walked back to the front of the house to find that the horses had been brought from the stables.

Kristina was waiting for him and she was wearing something on her head that looked like a boy's cap only made of velvet.

Because it was so hot she had taken off her riding-jacket and had arranged it carefully at the back of her saddle.

She looked lovely in a pretty muslin blouse inset with

lace and at the same time extremely young.

They mounted their horses and the Earl led the way though the park and on to the land beyond.

"This is where we can gallop," he told Kristina, "but be careful of rabbit holes. You will be fairly safe in the middle of the field."

They moved their horses forward as he spoke. He immediately became aware that Kristina intended to race him.

He realised she rode extremely well and he need not have worried about her on that account.

When they reached the end of the field he was only a nose ahead of her, because both their horses were so fit.

"That was delightful!" Kristina exclaimed. "I was never allowed to race so fast in Florence. And only when I have stayed with a friend have I been able to ride a horse nearly as good as this one."

"I am looking forward seeing those which you told me are yet to arrive."

Kristina thought for a moment before replying,

"If you are disappointed, then you must not be too polite to say so. I was thinking last night that if we are to be friends we must be honest with each other and I will tell you what I think is wrong."

"Yes, of course," the Earl agreed. "What would you like to complain about that I should be doing better?"

"I was not thinking of anything in particular, except that I think we should buy new curtains for the drawing room. I peeped in this morning and it is such a pretty room, much prettier than your study."

"I am intending to spend the money your father gave me on everything that is required on the estate first and the house will have to wait."

There was silence.

Then the Earl saw the expression on Kristina's face and he realised that he had spoken sharply.

He was just about to word it a little more tactfully when Kristina touched her horse with the whip she carried and it sprang forward. She shot through the gate and was galloping as fast as she could away from him.

Realising that she was upset, the Earl started to follow her as quickly as he could.

It took him some time.

Then as the field ended in an unjumpable and overgrown fence, Kristina was obliged to come to a standstill.

As the Earl drew up beside her he saw from the expression in her eyes what she was feeling.

"Forgive me," he said, "I did not mean to speak like that."

"You are – hating me again," Kristina murmured.

"Again?"

"I knew you were hating me – when we were being married. I could feel it vibrating from you – and that was why I knew I had to run away. But last night you were different."

"And I am still different now. Please forgive me. It was very selfish and thoughtless of me and I cannot do more than say I am desperately sorry."

He realised Kristina was looking at him as if to make quite certain that he was sincere.

Then as she gave a little sigh, he said.

"I have thought of a solution to this problem, which I had not expected."

"What is it?" she asked.

"I am going to leave the entire house for you to deal with. You can leave it as it is or you can re-decorate it as you wish. I will ask no questions and will try to make no comments."

"Do you really – mean it?"

"It is something I should have thought of earlier as I am sure you will make the house look as beautiful as I remember it when I was a small boy."

"Are you quite sure," Kristina asked slowly, "that is what you want me to do?"

"Of course it is – it is just that I was so stupid I did not think of it until I had upset you."

They were moving their horses slowly along the hedge towards a gate.

"I hate my money," Kristina said unexpectedly. "Suppose we give it all away."

"Of course we could, but I think you would find it rather uncomfortable without Brook or Martha and of course without the horses."

Kristina laughed.

"I thought you would have a good argument for keeping them if nothing else."

"Quite frankly," the Earl said, "I am too old to walk round the estate, and I would like to draw your attention to the fact that although we have ridden quite a long way we have not yet reached the first farm we have to visit."

"Then we will keep the horses – and of course the horses will need someone to look after them and food to eat just as we will. So perhaps we will not give away all my money after all!"

"It would be wise to keep some of it to buy your clothes," the Earl said. "You can hardly be like Lady Godiva and ride around naked!?

88

Kristina gave a little laugh and at the same time she blushed.

She looked so beautiful as she did so.

The Earl realised he had been rather shocking.

'I must remember how young she is,' he told himself again.

He must handle her very carefully and make certain he neither said nor did anything untoward to upset her.

CHAPTER FIVE

After they had visited the first farm, the Earl was becoming increasingly impressed by the way Kristina was conducting herself.

The whole situation had been very dramatic with the farmer and his wife almost in tears and then the atmosphere had changed miraculously from misery to joy as soon as the Earl had said a few words.

It was not surprising when they saw the dilapidated state of the farm itself and that the farmer's children were obviously underfed and poorly clothed.

Even the newly born calves were too thin and moved as if they were tired and listless and when the farmer finally grasped that things had changed, he reeled off a whole list of his requirements especially for livestock.

"You have run this farm for over fifteen years," the Earl had said, "and I trust you implicitly. I therefore leave it to you to spend what you need."

When they left, the farmer's wife was calling down a blessing from God on them.

Because they were affected by all the excitement, the farmer's children ran for some way beside their horses cheering them as they rode away from the farm.

The same happened at the next three farms and then they moved on to call on the villagers.

First of all the Earl called on an old man who had retired from being secretary and manager to his father and who had obliged him by undertaking the payment of the pensioners on that part of the estate.

He was lying on a bed in the living room when they entered his cottage.

He apologised because he was no longer able to get up and walk about.

"Stay where you are, Brent," the Earl said, "I have some very good news for you."

The Earl explained he could now afford to treble the pensioners' weekly allowances and to backdate them for six months.

Mr. Brent nearly fell off his bed.

"I cannot believe it, my Lord," he said, "and those on the estate who have suffered for so long will hardly believe it either."

"I feel the same," the Earl answered. "I know you will want to break the news personally to those who live here, and I have brought you a small present in gratitude for all you have done for me these past two years."

He had put two hundred pounds into an envelope which he handed to Mr. Brent so that he would not be embarrassed. He however guessed what it contained and was exceedingly grateful.

Looking round his very small cottage, the Earl saw that there were no luxuries and he was doubtful if Mr. Brent, like the rest of the people on the estate even had enough to eat.

When they rode on he said to Kristina,

"I told Brook we would not be back in time for luncheon, so we are going to stop at an inn which is only about half-a-mile further on."

"I have never taken luncheon – at an inn," Kristina replied, "so it will be something new for me."

The Earl was amused at how interested she was in the small black and white building. The inn stood on a village green and was called the *Pig and Whistle*.

The proprietor was almost overcome when he realised the Earl was to take luncheon with him and he and his wife hurried to see what they could provide for the meal.

The Earl and Kristina sat outside at a wooden table. It was where the elderly citizens drank their draughts of beer in the evening, when they could afford it.

Now the Earl learned from the proprietor of the *Pig and Whistle* that he had very few customers. He was even thinking he would have to shut up the inn because he could no longer run it profitably.

The Earl told him that he would pay for any repairs that were necessary and until the inn was back on its feet again, he need not pay any rent.

"In fact," the Earl told him, "because things are now better for me and I want you all to participate, I will pay you back three years rent to get you started so that you will be able to lay in larger supplies of beer and wines."

The proprietor was speechless, but his wife came out from the kitchen to tell the Earl over and over again that he had saved their home.

When they left she curtsied and kissed his hand and Kristina remarked to the Earl,

"Because these people are so grateful – and are crying with happiness – it makes me want to cry too."

"Don't you dare! I want women to smile and look pretty – they look so plain when they cry."

"You should really feel sorry for them – and want to wipe away their tears."

"I have done so in the past," the Earl said without thinking, "and it is something I did *not* enjoy."

There was silence while Kristina looked at him.

"Were they crying because – you were unkind to them?" she asked.

The Earl wondered whether he should tell her the truth. Then he thought it was good for her to gain some knowledge of the social world in which she was now living.

"To be frank," he answered, "they were crying because I was leaving them."

It was obviously an answer that Kristina had not expected. She puzzled over it for a moment before enquiring,

"You were leaving them – because you did not want to see them anymore?"

"Shall I say I had become a little bored."

"But they were not – bored with you," Kristina insisted. "So they wanted you to stay with them?"

"Just as you and I want to explore new countries, so I enjoy making new acquaintances."

She was quiet as they rode on.

"When you have come to know them," Kristina said after while, "you think you know all about them and so you ride away to find someone else who is even more exciting."

The Earl thought she had worked it out rather neatly so he replied,

"I am sure many women feel exactly the same. If you had a great number of young men running after you, you might soon find it monotonous and think there was someone better-looking and more interesting just round the corner."

He was speaking lightly but Kristina was obviously taking him seriously.

"I suppose it could happen," she mused, "if one was

single. But if one was married, it would be impossible to look elsewhere."

The Earl thought cynically that this was something which had not bothered a great number of women of his acquaintance.

He did not say anything and yet once again Kristina seemed able to read his thoughts.

"Are you – thinking," she said in a hesitating voice, "that after you have come to know me well – you might find me boring – and look for someone else?"

"I am not saying anything of the sort. When one is married one of course hopes that, as in the fairy story, one will live happily every after."

"But we have not started – by being happy.?

The Earl thought he was getting out of his depth in this conversation. He quickened the pace of his horse a little and replied,

"Now you have forgotten that we are two strangers who met only yesterday for the first time. We have only just become acquainted with each other and we are not really certain whether we like or dislike what we see. It really all depends on what happens today, tomorrow and for several weeks, months and years to come."

Kristina gave a little laugh.

"I do hope I am complicated enough for it to take all that time to discover me," she said, "but I have a feeling that – you are going to be very difficult."

"Why should you think so?" the Earl questioned.

"Because to begin with you are not what I expected you to look like. Nor have you behaved as I expected you to behave."

"I do hope that is two steps in the right direction, but I am curious to know what you thought I would look like."

Kristina looked at him with her head on one side like a little bird.

He felt her pose was exceedingly attractive.

"When Papa told me I was to marry an Earl," she said, "I thought he would be very proud, reserved and stuck-up with his own importance."

"I do hope I am not like that!"

"I thought too that he would be very severe-looking and would condescend to me and most people to whom he spoke and definitely would bully his servants."

The Earl laughed.

"I know very few Earls who behave like that, but perhaps one or two Dukes do when they grow old!"

"When you were so nice to the farmers and the proprietor of the inn," Kristina continued, "it was difficult to think of you as an Earl sitting in a high chair with a coronet on your head."

The Earl gave a longer laugh.

"If that is what you expect you are going to be disappointed. My coronet is in the safe and will not be taken out until I am asked to attend the next Coronation."

"I would like to see it one day – but I am very relieved you do not wear it."

"Now I know what you expected of me," the Earl replied, "it will make me feel as if I am not playing my part as I should and this thought reminds me that you have forgotten something very important."

"What is it?"

"That you are now a Countess and how do you suppose a Countess should behave?"

"I never imagined myself being a – Countess, but because I read so many fairy stories with my mother when I was a child – I did think that perhaps one day I would be a Princess."

"And that would be when you found Prince Charming and if I have to emulate him, who I remember in my books was a precocious but talented young man, I shall have to look to my laurels!"

Kristina did not reply.

He thought that any other woman would have declared that he was of course the Prince Charming of her dreams.

They rode on for a little while before Kristina asked,

"Where are we going now?"

"To another farm in another village which is the largest one on the estate and you will see the Church where I am told the steeple has collapsed."

"How could such a – terrible thing happen?"

"You know the answer – it is quite simply a lack of money. So before you think of giving away everything you possess, just imagine what you would look like if in a few years time you did not have a penny to your name."

He was speaking lightly but Kristina glanced at him quickly and then away again.

"Were you very unhappy because you were so poor?" she wanted to know.

"What I really minded was not being able to do anything for the people you have just met. But you saw how brave they were and how they struggled on despite the fact I could do nothing for them and every month of every year it grew worse."

"We must never let that happen again."

"That is what I hoped you would say, but I think if we are to do everything properly we shall have to spend a great deal of your own money, when the money your father gave me is exhausted."

"I thought that was what we agreed to do last night."

"But you have just made it clear to me that we are still strangers and I am frightened that if you find me boring or worse still unpleasant, you might run away again."

Kristina made a little gesture with her hands,

"I know now that last night – I was foolish. It was only because I was frightened of you – as *the Earl*. But now you have shrunk down – to a real person and that does make a big difference."

The Earl considered her comment for a moment before he said,

"I am delighted to be a real person, but perhaps I should really ask to be the Prince Charming of your dreams?"

Kristina laughed.

"He was not real and I think I knew even when I was quite small – that men were not really like him."

The Earl was not certain whether this was a compliment or not. At the same time he was aware that despite her childlike appearance, Kristina possessed an active brain.

She could put her thoughts into words in a way he had never expected. He found most women could talk of nothing but love when they were with him. Or else they would be complaining about quite trivial issues, which were of no interest to anyone except themselves.

He had always been certain that women read very little. Except of course the social columns of the newspapers and the magazines in which they would frequently see a photograph or sketch of themselves.

As they trotted on he enquired,

"I suppose you read quite a lot."

"Whenever I get the chance. We did have quite a good

collection of classic authors at the Convent. But I want to explore your library – just as I want to explore you."

"As an Arab would say – 'everything I have is yours'."

"Including your books, I would hope, but I must warn you that I am a very fast reader and when we can think of ourselves instead of others, we must fill up the shelves with every new book that is published."

"I shall be most interested to see what your favourite reading is. I have the idea that you were not allowed romantic novels in the Convent."

"No, of course not. Mother Superior would have been horrified at our reading anything so frivolous. Occasionally the girls were brave enough to smuggle in a novelette, but I much prefer history books and of course authors like Shakespeare and Charles Dickens."

"You will learn quite a lot from the latter about this new world into which you have been introduced and about which you know very little."

"That is what makes everything – so exciting."

She was looking around her as she spoke.

Again the Earl thought any other woman would have said it was he who made everything new and exciting.

'She is just a child,' he told himself again. 'Equally she has a very quick and alert brain. She would undoubtedly become bored with anything that was always monotonously the same.'

It was what he always suffered from himself.

He thought as they entered the village that this was the most extraordinary day he ever had ever known in his whole life.

The called at the shops where the Earl found, as he hoped, that Brook had paid all the long overdue bills.

They looked at the cottages which were all in need of

repair with holes in the thatch and windows cracked and every one of them needed painting.

Next they visited the Church.

The Earl had already learned that the Vicar, who had died after he had gone abroad had not been replaced. His father had not paid for a new one to take his place.

The Church door was open and so they walked in to find that there were holes in the roof where the tiles had fallen in and there was a mass of rubble in the pews.

The altar was still standing. As no one had taken away the gold cross, it was still there, as were the candles.

Although they were valuable, the Earl appreciated that as they were consecrated no one would be brave enough to steal them. It was traditional that bad luck would pursue anyone who stole from a Church for the rest of his life.

"How could the Church – have been left like this?" the Earl heard Kristina whisper beside him. "Where can the people pray – if they cannot come here?"

"I think they all pray for manna from Heaven," the Earl replied, "which now we are able to give them."

"The children have nowhere to be taught about God," Kristina added in a shocked voice.

"I realise that and so one of our first tasks will be to repair the Church and I expect that the Vicar's house will be almost as dilapidated. Then I will ask the Bishop to provide us with a new Parson."

"I cannot imagine anyone letting a place that is holy – falling into such a bad state," Kristina said.

"We will have it repaired at once and perhaps, as you know more about Churches than I do, you should supervise it."

He saw by the expression on Kristina's face that this idea had not occurred to her.

"I do not think I could," she said, "I might do something wrong."

"We will do it together – I know exactly how the Church looked when I was a small boy as I came here every Sunday with my mother. We will restore it as it used to be – as soon as possible."

"You understand – you *do* understand," Kristina exclaimed.

She spoke with a warmth in her voice which he had not heard before.

Equally it was obvious what she had been thinking, that because he was a typical aristocrat who had been thrust upon her by her father, he would only be concerned with the needs of the body and not with the soul.

They walked towards the altar.

As they reached the steps, Kristina suddenly knelt down. They were dusty and covered with chippings of stone from the fallen steeple.

She closed her eyes and put her hands together and the Earl could see that she was praying.

The sun coming through the window behind the altar shone on her golden hair as she had pulled off the cap she was wearing when they had been galloping.

He thought it would be difficult to find anyone who looked so lovely and she was obviously so very different from the beautiful women he had known in his past.

There was a childish innocent look about her as she prayed and it made it difficult for him to realise that she was indeed a woman and his wife.

He stood gazing down at her.

After several minutes she crossed herself and rose to her feet.

She smiled at the Earl quite unselfconsciously. She

was not, he thought, in the least embarrassed at having prayed in front of him. To her it was a completely natural way to behave in a Church.

She made a genuflection to the altar and walked past him.

It was as if she knew that their time in the Church was over and that they must return to the world outside.

They had tethered their horses to a fence which was broken in several places.

Without thinking the Earl put his hands round Kristina's waist and lifted her onto the saddle. It was only as he was doing so that he remembered that she did not wish to be touched.

She had made sure that at every place they had stopped there was a mounting-block.

Now as he sat her on her horse he did not feel her shrink away from him. He thought however, although he was not sure, that she held her breath.

He lifted the reins off the fence and placed them in her hands before mounting his own horse and they started to ride up the drive.

"We have done a lot of hard work today," the Earl said as the Hall came into sight. "I think we both deserve the excellent tea which I expect Brook will have prepared for us."

"We should not be hungry after such a nice luncheon, but I am greedy enough to say I am indeed hungry."

Kristina spoke quite naturally and the Earl thought that he had jumped one hurdle successfully. She was either unaware that he had touched her or perhaps was unaffected by it.

As they rode over the bridge the water was glittering in the sunshine and Kristina gave a cry and pointed down.

Coming from under the bridge were two white swans and behind them were three small cygnets.

"I am so glad they are still here," the Earl remarked. "I used to feed them when I was a child and I was afraid that when times were so bad that they would have flown away."

"Perhaps they flew back when they heard you had come home."

"It would be nice to think that is true, but we must have some more swans and that is another item to put on our list."

Kristina laughed,

"My list is already so long that you would be frightened if you saw it."

"We must both keep our lists private until we know each other better otherwise it will be embarrassing to accuse each other of being so extravagant!"

There was a silence until Kristina said,

"I understood today exactly why you wanted money from Papa – and I now realise that if you had not received it, many people would have suffered and been unhappy."

"I thought you would understand," the Earl replied in all sincerity.

A great number of women would have thought he was throwing money away to give so much to the poor instead of concentrating first on his own requirements.

Then before he could congratulate himself on having done the right thing, Kristina gave a cry,

"I had forgotten!"

"What is that?"

"The horses – they will have come today, I am sure of it."

She did not wait for the Earl to reply, but pushed her horse into a canter and rode across the courtyard and under the arch which led to the stables.

The Earl followed her, realising he had never given another thought to what she had said about the horses coming from Tattersall's.

Jim came running out as they appeared and he knew without being told that Kristina was right.

As she was ahead of the Earl she slipped off her horse and leaving him with Jim she ran into the stables.

"What time did the horses arrive, Jim?" the Earl enquired.

"Soon after you'd left, my Lord, and we've got some new help from the village which we'll need with so many new horses to look after."

The Earl did not wait to hear any more but walked into the stables.

Kristina was already in the first stall, gazing at a magnificent black stallion. It was the sort of thoroughbred he had often dreamed of owning, but thought would never be his.

Well bred and with a touch of Arab in him, he recognised that only those who could pay a very large sum could afford a horse that looked so fine.

Kristina was rushing excitedly from one stall to another and the Earl had to admit that he had never seen a better collection of handsome animals.

The groom from London and Jim were in ecstasies over them.

The Earl found that there were three new grooms from the village who were anxious to work in the stables. Two of them were experienced men while the third had been employed for a short time with one of the Earl's neighbours who was the Master of Foxhounds.

"The Colonel will be real upset, my Lord," the new

groom said, "when he hears you have horses like these. They be better than anything he has in his stables!"

"I feel very lucky to possess them and I am sure you will look after them well."

"I certainly will, my Lord," the groom promised.

The Earl was just about to turn away when he asked,

"Why did you leave the Colonel?"

The man hesitated.

"He has a nasty temper on him, my Lord," the groom said touching his forelock.

Some time later he persuaded a reluctant Kristina that they should go into the house for tea as it was now after five o'clock.

He thought that as they had been out all day she should rest. It seemed extraordinary to him that she was so small and so fragile in appearance, yet she could not only handle a large horse, but have complete control over it.

He considered as they walked up the steps that once again he had been very lucky. He might have been married to a woman who disliked horses.

She would then resent his being away from the house and her when he was riding around the estate.

Brook was waiting for them in the hall and Kristina said,

"The horses have arrived, Brook, and they are absolutely splendid!"

"I thought they would please your Ladyship."

"They are wonderful! I only wish we could tell Papa how grateful we are."

She did not wait for Brook to reply, but walked to the study where tea was waiting.

The Earl noticed that the room was very much cleaner

and tidier than it had been previously. There was an arrangement of flowers on each side of the mantelpiece and a bowl of roses in front of the window.

He knew that these changes were all down to Brook and he felt sure that Kristina would enjoy them and he was not mistaken.

"Flowers!" Kristina exclaimed. "How lovely!"

Then she looked at the Earl in rather a strange manner.

"What is the matter?" he asked

"I have just realised that I should have arranged the flowers for you. You told me to look after the house and Mama always arranged flowers for Papa in his sitting room. There were flowers everywhere because she loved him."

"Just as my mother did," the Earl said. "That is why I am determined to employ a great number of gardeners as soon as possible to make the garden as beautiful as it used to."

"And I will help you," Kristina added.

The Earl thought she looked like a flower herself, but he could not tell her.

She thanked Brook for thinking of the flowers when he came in with the tea and he said,

"When I was down in the village, I had not forgotten the garden, my Lord. There are two men who used to work here in the old days who are anxious to return."

"I hope you told them that they would be welcome," the Earl answered.

"With your Lordship's permission, they're starting work tomorrow morning as I was thinking you'd need almost an army to put things into shape before the summer's out."

"We will certainly engage an army if one is available. I intended to see to this tomorrow, but I am grateful to you for organising help so quickly."

As he spoke he remembered that once again everything had been done for him which he ought to be organising himself.

Where Brook was concerned he did not mind nor feel he was being pushed to one side. The man was obviously eager to be of use and he knew that he should encourage him.

When the cakes and scones came in, Brook was assisted by two footmen. Mrs. Brook must have worked very hard to produce so much so quickly.

He saw too that the footmen were already in livery. The Hunts must have told Brook that the old suits of livery had been stored upstairs in the attic.

As there were quite a number of them it would be easy for newcomers to be fitted in livery as soon as they arrived.

'Everything is improving,' he told himself, 'and it is far quicker than I expected, I can only be very, very grateful.'

Kristina was looking at the silver utensils on the silver tray. They were shining like mirrors.

"Would you like me to pour the tea?" she asked.

"Of course, that is something every hostess has to do."

"I hope I can do it as well as Mama used to, but we were never allowed tea in Florence. The nuns always said it was an English meal."

"Which is all the more reason for us to enjoy it," the Earl replied, "but if you eat all the cakes and scones I see waiting for us, you will soon be so fat you will have to buy a great many more clothes!"

Kristina laughed.

"Now you make me feel as if I am being naughty every time I eat any of that delicious-looking iced cake. And of course I will have to remember not to be too heavy in the saddle."

They were both laughing when the Earl sat down at the tea-table.

He thought how very different it was from the long silences of yesterday afternoon when they had driven down from London.

As he helped himself to hot buttered toast, he thought of his mother sitting where Kristina was now.

She would have wanted him to tell her everything that had happened today. What the people on the farms and in the villages had said to him and what he had said to them.

He had thought it was the sort of subject he would never be able to talk about with any other woman.

But Kristina, having given him his tea, was pouring out her own as she said,

"I was just wondering whether that last farmer, who was so thrilled when you said he could have as many sheep as he wanted, will buy the best breed."

"What makes you think he will not do so?"

"Papa always told me if one was buying anything it was wise to buy the best."

"Which is usually the most expensive," the Earl pointed out.

"Papa realised that, but equally he believed the best always lasted longer and in the case of animals it was always a good investment."

The Earl thought that this was an intelligent observation.

"I will certainly find out which is the best breed for our land and climate and I will suggest to Hopkins that is what he tries."

"I think it would be kind of you, after all I doubt if he can read, so he will not be able to learn about breeds except from others."

"Of course," the Earl agreed. "You are quite right and it is something I should have thought of myself."

"I have thought of something else you should do later when you have the time."

"That is just the important point – when we have time! What are you suggesting?"

"When I was at the Convent, one of the girls, who was French, was very excited because her father had taken up racehorses. He wished to challenge the English and was therefore building a racecourse near his Chateau on the Loire."

"A racecourse!" the Earl echoed almost beneath his breath.

"I thought it would be exciting for us to open one here and perhaps – if you built one it would bring more horses to the neighbourhood. It would certainly be interesting for the poorer people to watch. They have nothing to amuse themselves when they are not working."

Quite suddenly the Earl began to laugh.

"Why are you laughing?"

"Because as an explorer," he replied, "I have just discovered someone unique called Kristina who is quite unlike anyone else I have ever thought of, met or seen before!"

CHAPTER SIX

The Earl drove his team along the road at what he was certain was a record speed.

He had been to Oxford having received an urgent request from his Bank Manager and his Solicitors to visit them.

He thought perhaps the Solicitors would impart bad news about Mr. Randon and therefore he deliberately did not take Kristina with him.

However when he arrived it was to find that the summons was not bad news, but good.

A very large sum of money had arrived from America and his Solicitors and the bank were concerned as to how it should be invested.

They could not do anything without the Earl's instructions.

He realised that this extra money would make it easy for him to construct the racecourse Kristina was suggesting and even easier to achieve everything required on the estate.

He sent a large cheque to Lord Shield and promised him more when he needed it.

As the Earl drove back to the Hall, he was thinking that in the last three days Kristina had been so charming to the farmers and everyone they visited was entranced by her.

'She has the knack of getting on with people,' the Earl told himself, 'and that is most important on such a large estate.'

At the back of his mind was an idea that he might purchase more land, which would make his estate even grander and Cariston Hall more prestigious.

As he neared the village he drew in his team and they moved slowly past the thatched cottages which were now being repaired.

The Earl now employed a large number of workmen to carry out his orders – some were concerned with the Church whilst some were building a new school.

The rest were repairing and redecorating the cottages of the pensioners and making them as attractive as possible.

As soon as the Earl had returned and paid all his bills, the village general shop was bursting with more goods to sell than ever and the same applied to the butcher.

As the Earl was regarding the cottages he noticed that outside one of them was the chaise in which he had travelled to London.

He had told Kristina she could use it if she wanted to go anywhere as he intended to buy a new, small chaise to be drawn by two horses.

He thought too it would be a good idea to have a pony cart as it would make it easier for anyone in the house who wanted a run down to the village.

There were so many items for him to think about for all the improvements that sometimes he thought his head was whirling. It was impossible for his brain to concentrate on everything that was required.

He pulled in his horse to see that Jim was standing by the chaise.

"What has happened, Jim?"

"They comes to the Hall, my Lord, to ask us to find a midwife. The woman in this cottage were in labour and there be no one here to attend to her."

"Is her Ladyship inside?"

"Yes, my Lord. Us picked the midwife up some three miles away and brought her back post-haste."

"Look after the horse, Jim, I will go and see what is happening."

He handed Jim the reins and walked in through a gate which had already been repaired. He noted with satisfaction that flowers had been planted on either side of the flagged path.

The door of the cottage was ajar so the Earl opened it and looked inside.

There was no one in the kitchen, but there was however the sound of voices on the other side of the passage where he thought Kristina must be.

He was just about to knock on the door when a woman saw him and withdrew. He heard her say,

"His Lordship is here, my Lady."

The Earl waited.

A few minutes later, Kristina entered the room carrying a baby in her arms wrapped in a white shawl and she walked towards the Earl holding the infant very carefully.

"Here is a new member of your flock," she smiled. "You must admit he is a very good-looking baby."

As the child had only just been born, the Earl found it difficult to decide what his looks would be like in later life.

At the same time he was sure he had never seen anything quite so delightful as Kristina with a child in her arms. The scene made him think of the picture books of the

Madonna which his mother had read to him when he was a little boy.

As he looked at her, he found such an exquisite expression in her eyes that he knew in that instant that he was completely and unmistakably in love.

What he really desired was to see Kristina holding his own son in her arms and looking at him with the same expression on her face, which he recognised as the instinctive mother love of a woman for a child.

He realised it was something he had always been seeking, although he had not been conscious of it until now.

What he felt for Kristina at this moment was what he had always known in his heart he would feel one day for a woman.

But not for one who could ignite in him a fire which quickly burned itself out.

'*I love her*,' he thought, 'but she must not become aware of my feelings until I know that *she loves me.*'

Kristina raised her eyes from the baby.

"I was just thinking," she said, "that as this is the first baby born since you have started to restore the estate – I think you should be his Godfather – and he should bear your name."

"I would be very delighted for him to be called Michael if you think that will please his parents."

"I know that they would be thrilled and honoured," Kristina replied. "I will go and tell them."

She smiled at the Earl and moved into the next room and he thought he could hear a new note of excitement in the voices which had earlier been speaking quietly.

"They are overwhelmed at your kindness and Michael's mother says it is a very great honour," Kristina announced.

She came a little closer to the Earl and lowered her voice as she added,

"I think it will please the whole village and make them feel, as I know you want them to feel, that those who live on your estate are just one big happy family."

"How do you know that is what I want?" the Earl asked.

"At times I can read your thoughts and I felt it was what you were thinking."

"I shall have to be very careful what I think in the future."

Kristina laughed.

"I will not try to intrude, but I will know if you are thinking nasty thoughts about me like you were when we were married."

"That seems a long time ago," the Earl said, "and I have completely forgotten what happened."

"That is the right way to look at it and now let us go home. But first I must say goodbye to Michael's mother."

"I will go on ahead," the Earl said, "I have some instructions to give to the stables, but will join you as quickly as I can."

"Do not be too long."

The Earl walked outside and mounted his steed.

At the stables he found his head groom and two other grooms waiting for him.

The Earl had heard some importance news whilst he had been in Oxford. It was that a sale of horses would take place next week on the far side of the City.

He asked his head groom to find out more as if there was anything really good to be sold, it would be a mistake to miss it.

The head groom had quite a lot to say and it was some

time before the Earl could extract himself.

Jim had driven into the yard with the chaise and the Earl stopped for a moment to tell him how pleased he was with the way he had groomed the horses.

He did not want someone who had been faithful in the past to think he was being over-shadowed by all the newcomers.

Then he walked from the stables down to the courtyard where he saw to his surprise a closed carriage outside the front door. He wondered who was calling and hurried up the steps.

Brook was waiting in the hall and as he took his Lordship's gloves and hat from him said,

"Sir Geoffrey Hallet has called, my Lord."

"I wondered who it was and of course I am delighted to see him."

Sir Geoffrey had been a friend of his father's and his house and estate were only five miles away.

The Earl hurried towards the study which they were still using because the drawing room had not yet been redecorated.

He had almost reached the door when he heard Kristina scream and a moment later she ran out of the study almost bumping into him.

"What is the matter?" the Earl started to ask.

But she shot past him, running down the passage towards the hall.

The Earl entered the study.

Sir Geoffrey, as he expected, was standing in the centre of the room. He was a good-looking man nearing fifty whose hair was just beginning to turn grey. He was always a very cheerful, jovial person.

The Earl remembered him coming to the Hall ever

114

since he had been a child.

"This is a surprise, Sir Geoffrey, and I am so pleased to see you."

"And I am delighted to see you, my dear boy," he replied. "I only learned last night when I returned home from staying with a friend that you have been – married."

He rather hesitated over the last word.

Then before the Earl could respond he added,

"I am afraid, although I do not understand why, that I have upset your wife."

"What happened?"

"Well, I was quite overcome when I saw how beautiful she is, I knew of course you would marry someone lovely, but your wife is certainly exceptional."

The Earl did not speak, so after a moment Sir Geoffrey continued,

"I am afraid, although of course I had no intention of doing so, that I upset her."

"In what way?"

"I just said how glad I was to hear of your marriage and as I had known you for a verey long time, I thought the first thing I should do was to kiss the bride!"

The Earl drew his breath and now he understood.

It was just like Sir Geoffrey to ingratiate himself with a pretty woman. It was his cheerful and friendly way of behaving with nothing in the least sinister involved.

A kiss could never have upset an ordinary woman, but Kristina was not ordinary.

The idea of a strange man kissing her had forced her to scream and run away.

The Earl thought quickly before he said,

"I am sorry this should happen, Sir Geoffrey, but my

wife has suffered an unfortunate experience and at the moment holds a terror of being touched by a stranger."

"Of course I had no idea," Sir Geoffrey exclaimed, "and I apologise for distressing her in such a way. You must assure her that I just wanted to wish her every happiness as she is now your wife and I have known you for so many years."

"Yes, yes of course I understand," the Earl said, "and let me offer you a drink."

"I think I must have something to drink your health."

Sir Geoffrey accepted a whisky and soda and asked,

"I was told and I hope I am right, that your wife is the daughter of David Randon?"

"Yes, that is so, do you know him?"

"I have met him once or twice and thought him a most interesting man. As a matter of fact he married one of my relations."

The Earl became interested, realising, although it seemed extraordinary, that he had no idea of the name of Kristina's mother. It had not occurred to him to ask her.

"Who was it?" he enquired.

"Her name was Lady Elizabeth Norton and her father was the Marquis of Nortonford."

The Earl looked at him in surprise.

"Are any of her relations alive?" he asked Sir Geoffrey, "because I have not met any of them."

"They live in Yorkshire, my dear boy. I imagine the Marquis died a long time ago and I do remember hearing that Lady Elizabeth died in America."

"Yes, that is true, but I do not believe my wife has received any communication from the present Marquis of Nortonford if there is one."

"I believe the title has died out, although there may be a few cousins in that part of the world. It always seemed such a long way from here."

"That is true. Yet I think it would be nice for my wife to meet her mother's relations if they exist."

"I will try and find out for you," Sir Geoffrey offered. "I used to know one who married the daughter of my aunt. He must now be getting on in years and I have not heard from him for some time."

"Find out what you can, I know my wife will be grateful and so will I."

"I will do my best," Sir Geoffrey promised. "And you must bring your beautiful wife to dine with me. I cannot say my house can compete with yours, but at the same time, and this always annoyed your father, it is a hundred or so years older!"

The Earl laughed.

"I remember you both arguing about it and I wondered at the time why a hundred years should matter one way or the other."

"A man has to be proud of something and what could be better than his home?"

"You are quite right," the Earl agreed, "and I am very proud of mine."

"I see you are undertaking repairs and not before time, I might say. I can imagine you have a great deal to do."

"So much that I sometimes think the task will never be completed, but I have some new horses I would like to show you."

"There is nothing I should enjoy more," Sir Geoffrey said. "Perhaps I could call tomorrow or the next day. I cannot stop now, I have the Lord Lieutenant waiting to see me and you know how long-winded he can be."

"I remember my father saying the same!" the Earl laughed.

Sir Geoffrey walked towards the door and when they reached the hall, the Earl escorted him down the steps.

"Will you pay my respects to your wife," Sir Geoffrey said before he climbed into his carriage. "Tell her how much I regret upsetting her."

"It was a mistake and something best forgotten," the Earl replied a little sharply.

Sir Geoffrey patted him on the shoulder and stepped into his carriage.

The Earl shut the door and as he drove off he walked back in to the house deep in thought. Instead of going to his study he walked up the stairs.

He was sure that Kristina would have gone to her bedroom.

Without knocking he opened the door and walked in to find her sitting on the side of the bed.

When she saw the Earl she started and looked at him enquiringly.

The Earl shut the door behind him.

"I have come to ask you," he said in a harsh voice she had not heard before, "why you behaved to an old friend of mine like a foolish uncontrolled schoolgirl?"

There was silence before Kristina replied,

"He tried – to kiss me."

"How could you be so stupid?" the Earl asked. "Sir Geoffrey Hallet is an old family friend and has known me ever since I was a small boy. As he told me, he thought you extremely pretty and was paying you a compliment in suggesting that he should 'kiss the bride'."

Kristina did not answer, but the Earl noticed that she had gone very pale.

"Any woman who has any sense understands that if a man admires her, he pays her extravagant compliments and kisses her hand or perhaps, if he is elderly, her cheek."

He drew in his breath before he resumed,

"You cannot be so idiotic as to think there is anything sinister in what is a perfectly ordinary code of behaviour by an older man to a young woman."

"I did not – think it was like – that," Kristina murmured.

"Whatever you thought or did not think, you might try to behave like a lady. Can you imagine you mother screaming and running out of the room in such an over-dramatic theatrical manner? Incidentally Sir Geoffrey knew your mother and is actually a distant relative of yours."

"He knew – Mama!" Kristina managed to say.

"He knew your mother and he told me, as no one else bothered to do, to what a distinguished family she belonged. I cannot think she would be very proud of her daughter who has insulted an older man in a manner one would hardly expect from a guttersnipe."

Kristina gave a compulsive movement and then pressed her hands together.

The Earl saw there were tears at the back of her eyes. Yet she was still looking at him as if she was mesmerized and unable to look away.

"What you have to understand is that as you are married to me you have a certain position to maintain. Not only because it should come naturally to you as well-born and a lady, but also as an example to the people who look up to you and whose children will try to emulate you."

He paused for a moment.

"I am only thankful there was no one here from the village today to see the way you behaved. Get into your head once and for all that because God has given you a pretty face, quite a number of men will try to kiss you. You have to learn to accept it as a compliment, while being clever enough to prevent them from actually achieving their objective."

"Why should – they want to kiss a – pretty woman?" Kristina asked in a very low voice.

"Because if a man is a man and normal he finds a pretty woman irresistible and that is how life should be. Eventually he falls in love and if he is happily married his wife fulfils his dreams and other women no longer attract him. Until that happens he will find a pretty girl beguiling."

The Earl sensed as he spoke that this was a subject that Kristina did not know about nor understood.

He could almost see her thinking about it and turning it over in her mind.

Then she said,

"Did *you* want to – kiss me when you first – saw me?"

"If I had seen you for the first time at a ball or a party and had not known who you were, I would certainly have wanted to kiss you. As you know, we met under very different circumstances, and neither of us was in what one might call a normal position when we were married."

"Yes, I can – see that," Kristina said. "And I am – sorry."

The last word seemed to be almost dragged from her lips. As she spoke tears ran down her cheeks.

She looked so lovely that it was with the greatest difficulty that the Earl did not rush forward and take her into his arms. Every nerve in his body told him it was what he wanted.

But he knew it was too soon and he must wait.

He started to walk towards the door.

"Are you – very angry – with me?" Kristina asked in a voice he could hardly hear.

"No, not really," the Earl replied.

He left the room closing the door behind him.

Kristina covered her face with her hands. How could she make the Earl understand that she had acted purely impulsively?

She had been suddenly afraid of the gentleman who unexpectedly had put his arm round her and she had not stopped to think that he was old nor did it occur to her that he was just behaving like an elderly family friend.

'Oh, how could I have been so foolish?' she demanded of herself.

Now the tears ran faster down her face.

*

Later she was still feeling miserable, although she had stopped crying, when Martha came into the room.

"Oh, you're upstairs already, my Lady," she exclaimed. "I'll get your bath ready and tell one of the footmen to bring up the hot water."

Kristina walked towards the dressing-table so that the lady's maid should not see her tear-stained face.

"I've been hearing," Martha began as she laid the bath-mat on the carpet, "how His Lordship's given his name to Mrs. Robinson's new baby. Real kind of him that is and Mrs. Hunt says the whole village is thrilled at the news."

"I am sure they are," Kristina said in a muffled tone.

"But then his Lordship's always been a fine gentleman, Mrs. Hunt's been telling me how he struggled to help everyone when he hadn't a penny to his name, and how he never complained when there weren't enough to eat for a small rat let alone a fine upstanding young man!"

Martha paused for breath.

Kristina felt she must say something and murmured,

"It must have been very hard for him."

"Hard is not the right word for it. He struggled but it were too much for him. The house was falling down, the fields were untilled and some of the old people in the village was almost starving! It were terrible they say."

"I am sure it was."

"But now everything's different," Martha resumed in a satisfied tone. "And it's your Ladyship they're calling an angel who's come down from Heaven to help them and that's what you be!"

Kristina thought that at present she did not feel the least like an angel.

In fact she was so miserable she thought she would not go down for dinner.

But she wanted to see the Earl.

She wanted to be with him.

She wanted to talk to him and listen to what he had to say to her.

'He is not the least like the man I thought I had married,' she told herself. 'He is kind and thoughtful and I have failed him when I should have helped him.'

A footman entered with big cans of hot and cold water. Martha poured them into the bath and mixed them to exactly the right temperature before adding a bath essence which Kristina had bought in Florence.

When she had finished bathing, she dried herself with a towel which came from the linen cupboard and smelt of lavender.

"What does your Ladyship wish to wear tonight?" Martha asked.

Katrina walked to the wardrobe and chose one of the

prettier dresses she had brought with her from Florence.

It was white and ornamented with diamante. Its blue sash was the colour of Kristina's eyes and it was tied round her tiny waist with a big bow which fell down behind her until it touched the ground.

She hoped that perhaps the Earl would admire her.

Then as she looked at herself in the mirror, she wondered if he might want to kiss her.

He had said it was the biggest compliment a man could pay a woman and he had not yet complimented her in such a way.

'How could he when I tried to run away from him as soon as we were married?'

She thought now that she had been very stupid.

Her father had married her off to a man she had never met. At the same time because he loved her mother and her mother had loved him, he must have known the type of man with whom she would be happy.

It had not been entirely because of the Earl's title that he had seemed so suitable or that her father had known his father, but perhaps because he was extremely astute where men were concerned and he had known that the Earl was what she actually wanted in a husband.

She remembered her father saying that he never required a reference from anyone he engaged. He knew instinctively when he talked to them whether they were trustworthy and whether they would serve him as he wished to be served.

He had certainly used his intuition where the Earl was concerned.

'He is the right person for me,' Kristina mused 'and I was idiotic not to realise it as soon as I saw him.'

But she remembered she had been conscious of how

angry he was feeling while they were actually being married which was understandable.

Like herself the Earl felt no desire to be pitchforked into matrimony nor to be saddled with a wife he had never even seen simply because she had money.

'I have been foolish, very foolish!' Kristina was saying over and over again as she dressed.

Martha did up her gown at the back.

Then Kristina opened a drawer in the dressing-table and took out her jewellery-box, which she had not opened since she had married the Earl.

She had not been worried as to whether she looked attractive or not and yet tonight she wanted to look her best.

Her father had given her the jewellery belonging to her mother after she had died and had told her not to wear it until she was old enough to do so.

She had of course a few other pieces of her own – a pearl necklace, a pretty bracelet and a little diamond broach she sometimes wore on the front of her gown.

When she had returned to England she had felt no need to dress herself up.

But tonight she had made the Earl angry.

She knew she would not be able to sleep unless he forgave her and they were as happy as they had been during the last few days.

There had been so much to talk about and so much to occupy their minds and yet there were still a number of parts of the estate which neither of them had visited.

There were houses and cottages where they still had to call and they had not yet discussed the site for their racecourse.

"We will go to Royal Ascot this year," the Earl had said, "and we will not only look at the horses, but at the jockeys. A good jockey is most important if one wants to win races."

"Yes, of course," Kristina agreed. "I would love to go to Ascot. I have heard so much about it and how spectacular the meeting is."

"That is all a woman thinks about," the Earl teased. "You will be looking to see if your hat is better than everyone else's, while I watch the jockeys to see how they are riding."

"You know quite well that is what I shall be watching too," Kristina retorted. "But I think we should be more successful – if we rode our own horses."

"A woman rider at Ascot," the Earl exclaimed, "would undoubtedly make everyone, including the Prince of Wales, die of shock!"

"It would be thrilling – at any rate!"

They had both laughed at the idea.

But Kristina had not been conscious of the Earl's thoughts that because she was so beautiful, perhaps it would be a mistake for him to take her to Royal Ascot.

The Prince of Wales, as everyone knew, had a very roving eye. He had already caused a sensation in the social world by his love affair with Lily Langtry.

It was a question that the Earl had not asked himself and yet now he wondered what he would do if His Royal Highness showed an undue interest in his wife.

Lily Langtry's husband might discreetly disappear, but the Earl however appreciated that it was not something he could ever do nor would he tolerate the Prince flattering Kristina.

Aloud he said,

"I think we would be wise to keep Ascot for next year when we might be running our own horse."

"That would be even more thrilling!" Kristina

exclaimed. "Oh, please Michael, let us get ahead with the racecourse and begin to build our racing stable."

"We will definitely go to Newmarket for the next meeting," the Earl promised.

The Earl was beginning to make vague plans when he first realised just how rich he and Kristina now were.

When they had everything shipshape at the Hall, he might either buy or rent a house in London and they could become a part of the Social world in which every woman wanted to shine and most men found enjoyable.

It had never occurred to the Earl in the past that Society might be attractive as he knew only too well he could not afford it.

Now the world had become a different place.

Once their wedding was announced and everyone knew they were married, the invitations would roll in.

He would have to decide whether they stayed bogged down in the country or, in his own words, 'cut a dash' in Mayfair.

Every day he was with Kristina she seemed to grow lovelier and more glamorous and the real reason was happiness.

The Earl could imagine her turning the heads of every young man she met.

Inevitably, just as he would be present on the racecourse, the Prince of Wales would appear at the most important balls.

Perhaps, the Earl thought, he was exaggerating the danger as surely Kristina was really too young to attract him.

There was however no doubt that although she never bothered with her appearance, she was exceedingly beautiful.

He could not think of any woman he had met in

London who could eclipse her.

'If I was sensible, I would stay here in the country with her,' he told himself.

Yet was he really content to be with a girl who had only just left school, day after day, evening after evening?

But he realised that this was just what he really *did* want.

It seemed strange that he was happier than he had been for a very long time, in fact for three whole years.

And he recognised that it was entirely due to Kristina.

He loved her enthusiasm for everything that was happening, especially the way she laughed and her spontaneous joy over the simplest things which other women would have thought beneath their dignity.

To Kristina everything in life was exciting.

From the swans on the lake to the herb garden, which had been sadly neglected and of course the horses.

The Earl had to admit that while he enjoyed riding his magnificent new stallion, he enjoyed it twice as much when Kristina accompanied him.

They would race against each other.

If she could beat him, she was as excited and triumphant as if she had been awarded a medal.

Thinking it all over carefully he knew that he had enjoyed this past week more than anything he had enjoyed in his whole life.

And it was because he had fallen in love!

As he left Kristina's room and walked downstairs he felt that he had taken a risk in 'telling her off', as they would have said at school.

At the same time, he believed his words would help transform her from an unfledged schoolgirl into a woman.

She had appeared very womanly when she was holding the baby in her arms. The softness of her voice and the adoration in her eyes had not been that of a mere girl.

She had been a woman with deep feelings who was looking at the result of love.

'*I will make her love me*,' the Earl vowed as he strolled back to his study, 'if it is the last thing I ever do!'

He crossed the room to the window and looked out into the garden. The gardeners who had been working round the house had achieved miracles in a very short time.

The lawns had been cut and the flower beds tidied. Flowers had been planted where there had only been weeds. Because it was spring, the fruit trees were in full blossom.

'It is as pretty as a picture,' the Earl said to himself. What he was really saying in his heart was that it was almost as beautiful as Kristina.

Almost in spite of himself he was praying that one day she would be his.

CHAPTER SEVEN

Kristina took a last look at herself in the mirror observing that she had certainly made a difference to her appearance.

She was wearing a very pretty and valuable diamond necklace which had belonged to her mother and it matched the bracelets on her wrists.

In her ears, and it was the first time she had ever worn them, were small diamond earrings with pearls on each side, which made her look older, although they accentuated the translucence of her skin.

Feeling a little self-conscious she walked slowly down the stairs.

She was praying that the Earl was not still angry with her and she felt rather frightened that he may not join her for dinner.

She would dine alone.

It was a relief to see him standing in the study with his back to the fireplace. Even so she felt her heart turn a somersault and it must be because she was so nervous.

She had no idea how beautiful she looked as she stood hesitating for a moment in the doorway.

She walked towards the Earl.

"You are looking very smart tonight, Kristina," he said, "and may I add, very lovely."

He was speaking in his charming and alluring voice.

Kristina was so relieved that she felt like running towards him, but instead she forced herself to move with dignity until she reached him.

"Thank you for – the compliment. It is one you have not – paid me before."

"I have never seen you so elegantly dressed," the Earl replied. "I feel we should ask a number of dashing young men to serenade you and a band to dance to after dinner."

Kristina gave a little laugh.

"Perhaps we can do that one day – but the ballroom will need painting and decorating before we can invite anyone."

"We will do that once we have finished with the more important parts of the house," the Earl answered. "As you can see, the workmen have been erecting their scaffolding all day because they say they must start at the top."

"I was afraid the roof was leaking," Kristina said. "In fact there are a great number of tiles missing."

"I know that but now the workmen have started, you will be surprised how soon we shall be living in a palace rather than a house!"

At that moment Brook announced dinner.

"As you are dressed for the part," the Earl suggested, "I think I should offer you my arm."

He wondered as he spoke whether she would shrink away from him.

She placed her hand inside his arm without hesitating and they walked side by side into the dining room.

Almost as if Brook had guessed that it was a special occasion, there were extra candles on the table together with an elaborate arrangement of flowers.

Kristina clapped her hands.

"Oh, thank you Brook," she exclaimed. "How pretty you have made the table look!"

"I hoped you would be pleased, my Lady."

The Earl became aware that because the table was so brightly lit the rest of the room was almost in darkness.

He was sure that the servants, who always knew everything, had heard that there had been a quarrel and were determined that they should make it up in a romantic atmosphere.

It was something which, when he had first been forced into matrimony against his will, he might have found irritating.

Now he was touched because they were worrying over Kristina and him. He felt that sure his supposition was right when dinner was even better than anything Mrs. Brook had produced earlier.

There were four courses, each of them cooked to the perfection which he expected only from French chefs.

There was champagne for them to drink.

The Earl set himself out to make the meal amusing and memorable for Kristina and as her pretty laughter rang out frequently he knew that he had succeeded.

After desert which included strawberries from the garden the servants withdrew.

The Earl sat back in his chair.

He had accepted a liqueur which Brook had set beside him and Kristina was still sipping her coffee.

For a moment there was silence.

Then she said,

"That was a delicious dinner and I must tell Mrs. Brook so in the morning."

"The servants all try to please you, because you praise

them and they know you appreciate any effort they make on our behalf."

"They are very kind to me and they all think – you are wonderful. In fact in Martha's own words you are a 'fine gentleman'."

"That is praise indeed!" the Earl laughed.

"They mean it and you do behave exactly as a kind, caring landlord should to his people."

The Earl remained quiet for a moment before saying,

"You know that I can do so only because of you. If you were not here, the house would be about to tumble down and the Hunts and I would be sitting under a leaking roof with nothing to eat!"

"You must not think about it," Kristina said. "I think fate made you go – to my Papa at exactly the right moment and it is fate that is making everything we now desire come true."

"*Everything*?"

Kristina thought for a moment,

"I suppose because we are human beings we will keep asking for more. Perhaps if we are grateful enough – we will receive more."

"That is just what I am hoping will happen."

Kristina looked at the Earl questioningly wondering exactly what he meant.

He rose to his feet.

"Let us go into the study and I am waiting for you to tell me when I may look at the drawing room."

"The upholsterers have promised that they will bring the curtains tomorrow," Kristina answered, "and when the room is finished we must have another celebration."

"We certainly will," the Earl promised, "and perhaps

we will invite a number of people to come to dinner to celebrate with us."

Kristina did not pause but replied impulsively,

"I would much rather – be alone with you. It is *much* more fun – and we have so much to talk about."

"Then we will be alone," the Earl agreed quietly.

They reached the study where there were a great number of plans laid out on the desk for them to approve.

The head of the firm of builders repairing the house was anxious to restore parts which had been demolished over the centuries. He had even found some old prints and brought them for the Earl to inspect.

It was Kristina who had remembered that she had discovered some similar prints in one of the upstairs rooms. They were faded with age yet it was quite easy to see those parts of the house which had been removed.

Kristina thought it would be interesting and a distinct improvement if they were to be rebuilt.

The Earl was a little dubious at first, but by some gentle persuasion, eventually Kristina got her own way.

"We will go ahead if it pleases you," the Earl conceded, "but you do realise that we shall encounter considerable difficulties in restoring the statues which used to adorn the roof."

"I am sure almost identical statues could be obtained if we search for them," Kristina replied, "and if we tell the antique dealers what we are looking for they will doubtless find them for us."

They talked until Brook came in to ask if there was anything else his Lordship required.

It was then that they realised it was time they retired.

"You must see the head man tomorrow," Kristina said to the Earl, "and make sure he can find the right workmen for the job. I suppose they are the best firm available?"

"I am told that they are and they are certainly moving on quicker than I expected. I saw today that they have already erected the scaffolding at the back of the house."

"Yes, I know, it is outside my window and rather spoils my view of the garden."

"Then let us hope it will not be there too long."

Kristina looked at the clock and gave an exclamation.

"Do you realise," she said, "it is twenty minutes to twelve? It has been so fascinating planning what we will do that I had no idea it was so late."

"Nor had I."

Because they had been sitting side by side looking at the plans, the Earl had been vividly conscious that she was so close to him.

He longed to put his arms round her and pull her closer still. Yet he was well aware that she was talking to him with an ease and unselfconsciousness as if he was her brother.

'Or perhaps,' he said to himself, with a little twist to his lips, 'her father.'

He thought he had never seen her look more bewitching than she did tonight.

He noticed that when she gave him a sidelong glance, she was wondering whether he was still angry with her.

He had therefore gone out of his way to pay her effusive compliments, which were in fact the sort of compliments he had never paid to any other woman.

"You know I would value your opinion on this design," he had said as he passed her a print. "I am sure you are too intelligent not to realise that this is a fake," he said of another.

The eagerness with which she took what he was showing her and the sparkle in her eyes told him that she appreciated what he was saying.

What he really wanted to tell her was that she was too lovely for any man's peace of mind. And if no other man was allowed to kiss her, it was surely his right as her husband to do so.

He had however been in command of a great number of men when he had been in the Army. He had learnt to understand the character and personality of those whom he had commanded and there had never been a soldier he could not handle.

When women were concerned it had always been too easy. He had only to hold out his arms and they flew towards him like a bird going to roost.

He understood only too well that with Kristina he must not be hasty as she still needed to learn about love, something she had never known and never experienced.

He had to more subtle, more discriminating and more careful than he had ever been in his whole life.

'I love her,' he told himself, 'and one day she will love me. But I must not put a foot wrong. If I frighten her, I might lose her forever.'

He did not now believe that she would actually run away again, but she would creep back into her reserve and fear of men, which would make it impossible for him to approach her.

The Earl thought a little wryly that this venture was the most difficult task he had ever undertaken.

When he was a soldier facing a dangerous enemy he had used every ounce of his brain and brawn in the effort to defeat those he was opposing.

Now he needed to use his brain and his experience to make one young, innocent and very lovely girl give him her heart.

'I thought,' he mused, 'that trying to restore the Hall and the estate was a Herculean task. Now what I am confronting is an almost superhuman one!'

Kristina stacked the plans tidily onto a side table.

"It is so exciting to be building – a world of our own," she enthused, "and ordaining it just the way we want it."

"I agree with you, but we must not make any mistakes."

"No, of course not," Kristina agreed. "You are far too clever for mistakes."

"So are you and I can say this with complete sincerity, Kristina, that no other woman could be as intelligent and as creative as you."

"That is a very lovely of you to say so," Kristina exclaimed, "and I shall lie in bed tonight feeling a glow of warm satisfaction before I go to sleep."

The Earl extinguished the lights in the study with the exception of one lamp. As they walked towards the door he carried it in his hand.

"As soon as we have finished repairing the outside of the house, I am going to talk to you about installing electric light."

"I shall feel very up to date if we do," Kristina replied. "Even so there is something very romantic about the house as it is now."

It was Brook who in the last two days had put the candles into the silver sconces which he had cleaned and they now lit the hall and the passages.

Now as they reached the hall she thought how lovely the old furniture and the pictures looked in the light of just half-a-dozen candles.

The Earl was still carrying the lamp in his hand.

"You do not need that now," Kristina remarked.

"I shall need it in my bedroom, because to be honest I like reading by lamplight rather than the candles which Brook will have left for me."

"Wait until we install electric light," Kristina urged, "then if you want to read all night you can just switch it on."

"I can think of better things to do."

The Earl spoke without thinking.

It was the sort of remark which, if he had made it with his old friends or to any other woman, it would have evoked a knowing laugh and would doubtless followed by a witty rejoinder.

Kristina asked innocently,

"What sort of things?"

The Earl thought for a moment and then replied,

"It is at night that I have my best ideas, as I am sure you do."

"I suppose everybody does," Kristina responded seriously. "It is the one time when one is alone and not interrupted. I feel as if I am floating towards the sky – rather than worrying about the troubles and difficulties in my life."

They had reached her bedroom door.

As the Earl opened it for her she said,

"Thank you so much, Michael. It has been a lovely evening and we will talk more tomorrow."

"Of course we will."

As she moved her hand towards the door, the Earl took it and raised it to his lips.

He only just touched the softness of her skin.

As he did so he felt her quiver.

He hoped it was not with fear, but he could not be certain. Quickly he turned and walked away.

"Sleep well," he said as he heard Kristina's bedroom door shut behind her.

*

Kristina turned round to walk across her bedroom and as she did so she became aware that the curtains were blowing out from the windows.

There had been a slight wind during the day, but now with the darkness it had increased, although it was still a very warm night.

Kristina pulled back the curtains in case they should knock over anything on the nearby tables.

The stars were bright overhead and there was a moon moving up in the sky and what she could see of the gardens though the scaffolding appeared silvery in the moonlight and hauntingly lovely.

'I am sure that this one of the prettiest houses in the world,' Kristina said to herself. 'And how could anyone ask for more?'

She undressed herself, having told Martha not to sit up for her as she had admitted to starting a cough earlier in the day.

Kristina had told her to go to bed early and take something for it.

"That'll be honey, my Lady" Martha had said. "There's nothing like honey for a sore throat, as my mother told me when I were just a child."

"My mother said the same," Kristina replied. "You are not to worry, Martha. I can easily undo this gown, and I am sure tomorrow you will feel better."

"I hopes so, my Lady, and thank you for thinking of me."

Kristina hung up her dress in the wardrobe and took off her jewellery and laid it on the dressing–table. She thought she would put it back into its velvet boxes in the morning, although perhaps, as there were a number of workmen about, it would be wiser to keep it in a safe.

She knew Michael kept one in his bedroom.

'I could not bear to lose any of Mama's fabulous jewels,' Kristina told herself. 'I felt that when I was wearing them, she was guiding me and telling me how I should conduct myself tonight.'

The Earl was no longer angry with her as she had feared, but in fact, now that she thought about it, she had never known him so charming or so kind.

'He is a wonderful man,' she whispered as she looked in the mirror, 'and I would like him to think I am wonderful too.'

Then she remembered how cross he had been with her. She told herself that never, never again would she be so stupid or so foolish.

'He is quite right,' she murmured as she climbed into bed having said her prayers. 'I must behave in the way that Mama would and I am sure she is helping me.'

She blew out the candles by her bed having already extinguished those on her dressing-table.

The room was not in total darkness as the moonlight was coming in though the open window, casting a silver glow onto the carpet.

Kristina wondered if the Earl was watching the stars from his bedroom, before telling herself he would undoubtedly think it would sentimental to do so.

He was either going to sleep or reading a book.

'I must go to sleep,' she told herself, 'because there is so much to do tomorrow.'

She closed her eyes.

Then she heard a strange sound.

It was a creak, followed by a bang as if something fell hard had fallen to the ground.

She sat up in bed.

Then as the noise came again, she jumped up.

She was almost sure of what was happening and thought she must warn the Earl. Without thinking, she ran across the room just as she was in her nightgown.

She pulled open the communicating-door.

There was a boudoir between her room and the Earl's. It was more of an alcove and very intimate and was where his mother had written her letters and kept her most prized and cherished possessions.

Like the presents her husband and son had given her on her birthdays and at Christmas. There was a collection of Dresden china angels she had accumulated over the years.

Kristina crossed the boudoir and pulled open the door on the other side which led into the Earl's bedroom.

She saw that he was in bed with the small lamp beside him reading a book.

He looked up and exclaimed in astonishment,

"Kristina! What is it?"

"I think the wind is – knocking down the scaffolding," she told him breathlessly. "It is making strange noises – and if it collapses it could do a great deal of damage to the windows below."

The Earl closed his book.

"I will come and see to it," he said firmly.

Then he hesitated before he added.

"To save your blushes, I suggest you look the other way while I get out of bed."

Kristina did blush as she turned round to stand in the doorway of the boudoir with her back towards the Earl.

Because it had been so warm he was naked to the waist.

When he climbed out of bed he pulled on a silk robe which Brook had left on a chair and picked up the lamp.

"Now I am ready, so let us look at the damage. I shall be extremely annoyed if they have erected the scaffold so carelessly that it can be blown about by the slightest wind."

He moved towards Kristina as he spoke and she walked into the boudoir and as he joined her she let him go first because he was carrying the lamp.

He crossed the room and pulled open the communicating-door into her bedroom which she had left ajar and entered the room with Kristina close behind him.

They both came to a standstill.

Standing in the bedroom by the open window through which he had obviously just entered was a man.

He was dressed in black and to Kristina's horror he wore a black mask over his eyes. On his head was a cap pulled so low that it was impossible to see his features.

"What are you doing here?" the Earl demanded sharply, holding up the lamp.

As he spoke the intruder took a revolver from his pocket and pointed it at him.

"I wants all the money you 'ave."

He spoke with a strong accent which the Earl thought was Cockney.

"I don't have any money with me."

"Then you'd better git it," the man said, "an' if you don't you'll find it very uncomfortable to 'ave a piece of lead through your 'eart."

He was still pointing the revolver at the Earl's chest as he spoke.

Kristina gave a cry of horror.

The intruder turned his attention to her.

"As for your pretty lady," he snarled, "you can give I that jewellery you 'ave on your dressing-table."

Kristina looked at the Earl.

To reach the dressing-table she had to pass him and the burglar and for the first time she realised she was wearing only her nightgown.

The Earl was wondering desperately what he could do.

He was holding the lamp in his left hand and although his right was free, he was some distance, perhaps eight feet, from the man pointing the gun at him.

If he made a hasty movement he could be shot long before he reached him and then it would be impossible for him to protect Kristina.

Almost as if the burglar knew what he was thinking, he growled to Kristina,

"Do as I tells you or I'll finish orf 'is Lordship afore I makes you give I what I wants."

"How – can you be – so wicked?" Kristina asked.

The burglar laughed and it was an unpleasant sound.

"The answer to that be quite simple, I be poor an' you be rich an' I wants a bit of comfort in me old age!"

"Suppose I give you some money," the Earl suggested coolly, "and you leave my wife's jewellery where it is. It belonged to her mother and she has no wish to part with it."

"Well my mother left I nothin'. So I'll 'ave the jewels as well as your money, which I knows be in your bedroom in a safe, so you can't deceive I."

As he realised that the Earl and Kristina were just staring at him he said,

"Come on, I ain't goin' to wait all night. Give I the jewellery or I'll 'elp meself to it and anythin' else I wants. A dead man won't be able to stop me!"

He waved his revolver even more menacingly at the Earl.

Kristina again gave an anguished cry of horror.

She ran behind the Earl to her dressing-table, so as not to be near the burglar.

She picked up her mother's jewellery – the necklace, the bracelets and the earrings. They glittered in the light from the lamp as she turned back towards the burglar.

"That be more like it," he said as she approached him.

He held out his left hand.

As he did so Kristina raised her leg.

Quite suddenly without any warning, the burglar fell backwards on to the floor with a crash.

His arms were stretched out and the revolver dropped from his hand and fell a foot or so away from him under a chair.

With the swiftness of a man who had often been in danger, the Earl dashed forwards to pick up the revolver. At the same time he put the lamp which was encumbering him down on the nearest table.

Even as he did so the burglar scrambled to his feet and like a frightened animal he just seemed to dive through the window.

He must have fallen onto the scaffolding and the Earl could hear his footsteps running on the boards.

He was about to run to the window when Kristina moved.

She dropped the jewellery on the floor and flung herself against him.

"He might have – killed you," she cried incoherently.

Her arms encircled his neck and she kissed his cheek.

Then her lips touched his.

The Earl put his arms round her pulling her close against him.

He kissed her fiercely, possessively and passionately.

He kissed her until she felt as if she melted into him and they were no longer two people but one.

The terror she had felt at thinking he might be killed had vanished into a wild uncontrollable excitement.

It was a rapture she had never known or imagined possible.

The moonlight was seeping though her body and the stars were twinkling in her breast.

Her arms round the Earl's neck tightened and she moved even closer to him.

His robe had fallen open and he could feel her heart beating against his naked chest. He thought it was the most wonderful feeling of his entire life.

He had kissed many women but he had never known a kiss that was so utterly perfect, so completely ecstatic.

It made him feel as if he was carrying Kristina into the sky and they were no longer human.

Only when they were both breathless did he raise his head and look down at her.

Her golden hair was falling over her bare shoulders.

The light from the lamp showed him that love had transformed her and she was lovelier and more beautiful than any woman he had ever dreamed about.

"I love you," he said and his voice was very deep.

"I love you – I love you," Kristina whispered, "and I thought he was going – to kill you, but he has gone away."

"Let him go," the Earl said. "I have found you and that is all that matters."

He kissed her again.

It was impossible for him to put his feelings and emotions into words. The miracle had happened and *she actually loved him*.

Although her lips were soft, sweet and innocent, he sensed that there was a rapture behind them.

It could come only from a love which echoed his own.

When he raised his head again he asked her,

"How could you have been so brilliant as to know about jujitsu when there was nothing I could do?"

Kristina laughed,

"There was a Japanese girl at the Convent in Florence – and she showed us how to defend ourselves."

"So you saved both of us."

"I was so very frightened – that he might shoot you," Kristina sighed.

"Why?" the Earl asked as he wanted to hear her answer.

"Because I love you," Kristina whispered. "I love you with all my heart – and with all my soul as the nuns said I should do when I find – the love of my life."

"Are you quite sure?" the Earl asked.

Kristina moved a little closer to him.

"Quite, quite sure," she murmured.

"In which case," he replied, "it is unnecessary for us to stand here."

He lifted her into his arms and carried her across the room.

He laid her down on the bed with her head on the pillows.

"I do not want you – to leave me."

The Earl smiled.

"I have *no* intention of leaving you."

He sat down on the bed beside her and pulled her into his arms.

"If only you knew," he said, "how much I have longed for you to tell me that you love me. It has been an agony I hope never to experience again. To know you were only a room away from me and I dare not come near you."

Kristina pressed her lips against his cheek.

"How could I have been so foolish," she asked, "as to not to allow you – to touch me as you wanted to?"

"Of course I wanted to," the Earl replied. "I wanted to kiss you and to make you mine."

He realised what he had said.

In a different tone he continued very quietly,

"I do not want to frighten you, my darling."

"I will never be frightened of you again. I was so afraid – when you were angry with me that you would want – to leave me."

"I will never leave you and I will never allow you to leave me. I love you, my precious little wife, the same way as you love me, with all my heart and all my soul."

He kissed her gently before he added,

"I think *now* we can really start our marriage and be very, very happy."

"I love you so so very much," Kristina murmured.

The Earl kissed her and she thought nothing could be more wonderful than the touch of his lips.

His arms were now entwined around her and she realised, although she did not really understand, that he wanted more.

"I am yours completely and absolutely yours," she whispered, "but I know that I am very ignorant."

The Earl did not speak and she continued,

"Please teach me – about love. Teach me to do – what you wish me to do, because I am – so frightened of disappointing you."

Kristina drew in her breath.

"If you had the chance to start all over again – and not have to worry about money," she asked, "would you still want – to marry me?"

"I would want to marry you if you were rich, poor or even destitute," the Earl answered. "You are mine, because you are perfect, and because you are the woman I always felt was waiting for me somewhere if I could only find her."

"Papa was always clever, so very clever and he knew what was best for both of us."

"I only hope he realises how happy we are," the Earl breathed. "I love you, my darling and now I am going to show you how much."

He kissed her passionately as he spoke and there was no further need for words.

As he kissed her and did not stop kissing her, she felt he was carrying her up into the sky.

The room enveloped them and the stars were on their lips and in their hearts.

Kristina felt as if the Heavens had opened and the angels were singing.

This was love.

A love which comes from God and which all mankind seek but only a few are lucky enough to find.

It is the love of the heart and the soul and is in itself perfect.

The love which never dies, but carries on into eternity.

WS - #0159 - 070823 - C0 - 198/129/9 - PB - 9781905155262 - Gloss Lamination